The corners of Garrick's lips twitched into a smile. He reached for the baby.

This wasn't exactly the kind of emergency he had in mind when he bolted over here, but it was a job that still needed to be done.

Garrick nestled the little girl in the crook of his arm. As he swayed back and forth, the baby quieted down. "That's a good girl," he cooed.

"How did you do that?" his neighbor asked wide-eyed.

"I've been told I'm a natural with babies and animals," he boasted proudly.

"You're a godsend."

The woman raked her fingers through her hair—something she should stop doing, he noted.

"Yeah, well, I guess if you just get us a new diaper, I can help you change her and then I'll get out of your hair." He didn't mean to mention her hair, but it had a way of drawing the eye.

She blinked. "A diaper?"

ADRIANNE BYRD

has always preferred to live within the realms of her imagination where all the men are gorgeous and the women are up to all the challenge of whatever trouble they manage to get into. Her first Kimani Press release, *She's My Baby*, was inspired by a true-life incident. Ms. Byrd's youngest sister politely informed her that she was having a baby—ten days before her due date! Her little sis and baby moved in. They've been living with Ms. Byrd happily, *temporarily*, ever after.

Adrianne Byrd

She's
My Baby

KIMANI
ROMANCE

For my niece Courtney Breanna White
I hope I don't screw this up

 KIMANI PRESS™

ISBN-13: 978-1-58314-779-5
ISBN-10:   1-58314-779-9

SHE'S MY BABY

Copyright © 2006 by Adrianne Byrd

All rights reserved. The reproduction, transmission or utilization
of this work in whole or in part in any form by any electronic, mechanical
or other means, now known or hereafter invented, including xerography,
photocopying and recording, or in any information storage or retrieval
system, is forbidden without written permission. For permission please
contact Kimani Press, Editorial Office, 233 Broadway, New York, NY
10279 U.S.A.

All characters in this book have no existence outside the imagination of
the author and have no relation whatsoever to anyone bearing the same
name or names. They are not even distantly inspired by any individual
known or unknown to the author, and all incidents are pure invention.
Any resemblance to actual persons, living or dead, is entirely coincidental.

® and TM are trademarks. Trademarks indicated with ® are registered in
the United States Patent and Trademark Office, the Canadian Trade Marks
Office and/or other countries.

www.kimanipress.com

Printed in U.S.A.

Dear Reader,

I hope you enjoyed Leila and Garrick's story. I have to admit that it was one of my easier subject matters to write about since I positively break out into a cold sweat every time my sister even hints for me to babysit my one-year-old niece. Some women, like me, really have to work to dust off unused maternal instincts. Like Leila, I discovered that even after sleepless nights, countless diaper changes and constant worrying, there is a unique joy in being around a baby. Nothing gives you the same kind of pleasure as when a child smiles at you. So much so that you find yourself doing the most ridiculous things—like "goo-gooing" while you're holding up the line at the grocery store—just to win another toothless grin.

So, now I have a baby at the house...all I have to do is keep peeking out the window to find my Garrick Grayson.

It could happen...

Chapter 1

Leila Owens, founder and editor director of *Atlanta Spice* magazine, gaped at the world's greatest assistant—her assistant—and her good friend and prayed that her ears were clogged with wax. "You're pregnant?"

"Yes. Isn't it great? The news is kind of an early Christmas gift to my family." Ciara Winston beamed a radiant smile as she closed Leila's office door and journeyed into the room.

"Nooo," Leila half moaned, half groaned, and then dropped her head into the palms of her hands. "Why on earth would you go off and do something so…silly…and suicidal?"

"Silly and suicidal?"

"Babies are career killers in this industry," Leila snapped, jerking her desk drawer open to grab the industrial-size bottle of Rolaids. "They need constant attention, they are always sick, and they are always crying for something."

Ciara crossed her arms. "Babies aren't the only ones who do that."

"I can't believe you're doing this to me," Leila added as she popped a few pills into her mouth.

Her assistant laughed, but when Leila's sharp gaze stabbed her, Ciara sobered. "Leila, this has nothing to do with you."

"Doesn't it? What do you think is going to happen to me while you're off having morning sickness, water-retention issues, and raging mood swings? I have a company to run and I can't do that without my right-hand woman at my side. I *need* you." Leila downed two more tablets for good measure.

"I'm not dying. I'm just having a baby." Before Leila could respond, Ciara held up a silencing finger. "Please, let me finish before you say something that will cause me to turn in my resignation." She lowered her hand.

Leila clamped her mouth close.

"Elmo and I—"

"Elmo. What kind of name…"

Ciara jutted her finger back into the air and Leila grudgingly fell silent again. "Look, don't get all neurotic on me. I like you. I'm also insane enough to say that I like working for you. But I am ready for the next chapter in my life—motherhood. Now, the polite thing for you to do is to congratulate me."

Leila ground her teeth and then lowered into her chair.

"I can be just as stubborn as you and I can stand here all day."

It was true, Leila knew. Her assistant's bull-headedness was one of the reasons that made Ciara a perfect match for Leila. Yet, for every common denominator between them, there were five differences. This whole family-and-marriage thing was just another example.

Ciara cleared her throat and waited.

"All right, all right. Congratulations. I hope

you and *Tickle Me Elmo* have a slew of rug rats, if it makes you happy."

"Thank you." Ciara smiled sweetly. "I knew you had it in you. One day I hope you will experience the joy of marriage and children."

"Spare me." Leila leaned back in her chair. "And don't think I'm going to suffer through 'children are great' sermons from you on a daily basis. Not all single women are miserable. *Atlanta Spice* is my marriage and I'm completely happy with it."

"If you say so." Ciara pivoted and headed back out. "By the way," she said, opening the door. "Your sister called this morning. Twice."

Leila reached back into her drawer-slash-personal-pharmacy for some antacids. "Which sister?"

"Roslyn. Said it was important."

"Everything is important to her. Thanks… and can you see about getting me some aspirin? I'm running low."

"You got it," Ciara laughed and finally made her exit.

Leila, meanwhile, placed mental bets with herself on when Ciara would quit. She could hear it now: *Elmo and I agreed that I should become a full-time mom.* That's what all twenty-something women wanted to do nowadays.

Disgusted, she reached for the phone and punched in Roslyn's number. She sidelined her magic pink pills until she heard what her sister had to say. On rare occasions important issues weren't so bad.

"You have to be the hardest person in the world to get on the phone," Roslyn launched into saying.

"Well, hello to you, too."

"Sorry. Hello. Have you heard from Samantha?"

"No." Leila snatched up the Pepto. "Should I have?"

"She's missing."

In any other family those words might sound off an alarm; but not with the Owenses, and not when the missing person in question was Samantha. "Sam is not missing. Sam just failed to tell anyone where she's going—as usual. No big deal. She'll turn up." *And hopefully not at my place.*

"I'm not too sure. I've been calling her new

apartment out in Las Vegas for two weeks. Finally, I reached one of her neighbors, Ms. Friedman, and just found out some disturbing news—"

"Ms. Owens, we have a problem." Deonté Stylianos, her photo director, jetted into the room, red-faced and wild-eyed.

Leila lowered the phone and placed a hand over the mouthpiece. "What is it?"

"Erika hasn't turned in the photos of the Laura Biagiotti collection. Those were set to go to the printers by five."

Leila glanced at her watch and jumped to her feet. "It's four. Why am I just now hearing about this?"

Deonté sighed. "I covered for Erika when she missed the first deadline because she swore to have the pictures to me in time for the printers."

"Damn it." Leila pressed the phone back to her ear. "Roslyn, I have to go. I have a *real* emergency to deal with right now."

"But, Sam had a—"

"I'll call you back. I promise." Not waiting for a response, Leila hung up.

Roslyn exhaled a long frustrated breath and returned the phone back to its cradle.

"What did she say?" Patrick asked.

Roslyn frowned as she glanced over at her husband. "I didn't get a chance to tell her. She had to go."

Patrick flashed his deep-pitted dimples as he moved next to her and draped a strong arm around her waist. "Honey, maybe you're making a big deal out of nothing? This isn't the first time Sam has pulled a stunt like this."

"I know, but this time it's different. There's another life involved."

"We don't know that for sure. Ms. Friedman could've been mistaken. Sam could have been babysitting a friend's kid for all we know."

He had a point; but as Roslyn thought about her sister's elderly neighbor, doubt crept over her. "I don't think we should go on our trip until we get to the bottom of this."

"You're joking." Patrick's body deflated as his arm fell from her waist. "We've been saving for two years to go on this trip. Barbados in December—you said it would be a dream come true."

"I know, I know, but this thing with Samantha." She shook her head. "Something's not right. I can feel it."

"Nothing is ever *right* with Sam. She pulls these little stunts for attention. You know that."

She did.

As if sensing he was making some headway, he drew her close again. "The tickets are non-refundable and the kids are excited. Besides, if there is a real emergency, Leila is more than capable of handling it."

That was true as well. Leila's tough-love tactics always worked better than Roslyn's *please let me try to fix everything for you* strategy.

"You're right." Roslyn smiled, laying her head against her husband's broad chest. "If anything is wrong, Leila will handle it."

Chapter 2

"Lord, save me from gold diggers and career-driven women," Garrick Grayson prayed into his glass of eggnog before he downed it in one long gulp. At the very least he'd hoped to drown out the overly cheerful song "Jingle Bell Rock" that blasted from every speaker in his brother's house.

"Hey, bro. You better ease up on that. I have no intentions of carrying you out of here with my bad back."

Garrick flashed Orlando a wounded look.

"It's been a bad day. Indulge me." He glanced around his brother's crowded Christmas party.

Orlando shook his head. "This is about Miranda, isn't it?"

"I stopped drinking over Miranda two years ago. This is about me perfecting the fine art of screwing up my life. I'm forty-five years old and I haven't accomplished anything meaning-ful."

"Ooh. It's going to be one of those even-ings?"

"C'mon. You know it's true."

Orlando laughed. "I don't know any such thing. I know you're a man with the Midas touch when it comes to wheeling and dealing, which is why Dad left the family business in your capable hands. God bless him."

Garrick studied his brother. "You don't feel slighted?"

"Heavens no." Orlando laughed with genuine amusement. "I'm no architect and I don't enjoy pushing paper around. The football field is where I belong."

Garrick smiled at the truth of Orlando's words. His brother had never made it past college ball, but he was just as happy coaching his beloved junior-high-school team.

Tamara, Orlando's beautiful full-figured wife, looped an arm around her husband, and then leaned lovingly into him. "You're supposed to be mingling."

"I am." Orlando delivered a quick peck against her voluptuous lips. "I'm making sure this bum you invited doesn't guzzle all the eggnog."

Tamara turned her glowing smile toward Garrick. "He's harmless…and so is the eggnog. No alcohol."

"I knew it tasted funny," Garrick joked.

Sliding gingerly from one brother to the other, Tamara planted a kiss against Garrick's cheek. "Merry Christmas, Garrick."

"Merry Christmas, gorgeous."

"How's the new house?" Tamara asked.

"I'm enjoying it so far. Of course, I've only been there a week. But it seems like a nice *quiet* neighborhood."

"Why didn't you just build another house? You do such great work."

"It's a transitional house and it's just me." He shrugged.

"Then maybe I should come up and see you sometime," she said in her best Mae West imitation.

They exchanged a few minutes of harmless flirtation—just long enough to playfully stir Orlando's jealousy.

"Okay, that's enough." Orlando pulled his wife back to his side. "Me Tarzan, she's Jane."

"Oh, are we playing that one tonight?" Tamara murmured against her husband's ear and slid her arm around his waist.

"I think I can dig up my leopard-print loincloth."

"Hello. I'm still standing here," Garrick reminded them.

The mushy husband-and-wife team chuckled. However, the duty of playing hostess called and, with a great show of reluctance, Tamara glided out of Orlando's arm.

"I'll leave you two alone, but, honey, don't forget to mingle."

"You got it."

Garrick ladled another cup of eggnog as he watched his sister-in-law vanish into the crowd. "I envy you," he blurted.

Orlando's smile turned sly. "I know."

Garrick chuckled, but his mood darkened in the next instant when Bing Crosby vowed solemnly that he would be home for Christmas. "Miranda is getting married again."

"Tamara told me. Some doctor or another, right?"

"Yeah."

Orlando fell silent for a moment, glanced around to make sure no one was listening, and then asked, "Are you still in love with her?"

"I'll always love her," Garrick admitted in a voice laden with emotion. "But, no. I'm not *in* love with her."

"Tamara said she's pregnant."

Garrick lowered his head as he clenched his drink. The news hurt just as much the second time around. "Yeah," he croaked.

During his seven-year marriage to Miranda, Garrick had waited, prayed, and then begged to start a family with his ambitious ladder-climbing wife. However, the answers were always: after this next deal, after this next trip, and after this next promotion—they were all deviations of the word *no*.

"It just means that it was never meant to be," Orlando said, and then winced. "I didn't mean it like that. I mean—"

"It's okay. I know what you meant." Garrick sighed and backed away. "Forgive me, but the last thing I want engraved on my tombstone is how I was a whiz at business. I want the same thing Dad has and you'll have. Here lies a great husband and a wonderful father. I want a real legacy."

"You'll get those things, bro." Orlando met his brother's direct gaze. "I know you will…because Tamara and I have already lined up the perfect woman for you."

Garrick groaned. "Tamara set me up with Miranda, remember?"

"Trial and error." Orlando shrugged. "On all our parts. So what do you say?"

"Is she here tonight?" he asked, unable to keep the dread out of his voice.

"Nah. You know I wouldn't land a sneak attack on you like that."

Garrick's eyes narrowed.

"All right. She was here earlier, checked you out, and gave us the okay to pass you her number."

"I was under surveillance and you didn't tell me?"

"Tamara told me not to. So what do you say?"

"I say you've been married too long and have forgotten the brothers' allegiance."

"Yes or no?"

Garrick weighed his options, thought about his love life that was on serious life support, and then caved. "All right…on one condition."

"I know. I know. No gold diggers and no career women."

Garrick smiled. "You got it."

On Christmas morning, Leila stretched languorously in her eastern, king-size Italian bed and gave serious thought to staying put for the entire day. Why not? With Roslyn and her family in Barbados and Sam living it up in sin city, she was actually going to be alone for the holidays.

"Peace and quiet," she moaned, curling back up against a pillow.

The phone rang.

Leila laughed as she crept an arm out toward the nightstand. "Hello?"

When no one answered, she frowned and made a concerted effort to suppress her irritation. It was Christmas, after all. Dropping the receiver back onto its cradle, she once again prepared for another flight to dreamland.

The phone rang again.

Spewing a string of curse words, Leila snatched off her night mask and grabbed the phone.

"Hello."

The caller didn't respond, but Leila could make out someone breathing—no, crying—on the other end.

"Who is this?" When the caller refused to speak, Leila's sixth sense tingled to life. "Samantha?"

The caller hung up.

Leila held the phone. What kind of game was Sam playing now?

Huffing out a tired breath, Leila finally hung up the phone and climbed out of bed with all her dreams of spending the day in bed gone. Her mind was still wrapped on the strange call as she donned her robe and slipped into her favorite pair of slippers.

If she had any hopes of figuring out the new game her baby sister was playing, she would need her morning coffee—preferably a full pot.

Midway down the stairs, the sound of music caught her ear. She stopped.

Had she left the stereo on? Wait, she hadn't listened to it last night. Her heart skipped a beat until she thought of the unlikelihood of a killer sneaking into her place only to play… "Rock-a-bye Baby."

"Hello?" She crept down to the landing, trying to convince herself she was naming the wrong tune. As she followed the music, her confusion grew. It was coming from the kitchen.

Her usually dependable creative imagination had drawn a blank on what awaited her; but nevertheless, she put on a brave front and continued placing one foot in front of the other.

The moment she entered the kitchen, her gaze zeroed onto a frilly pink bassinette in the center of the kitchen table.

Leila blinked. When the image remained, she blinked again. It was still there and the looped music reverberated off the walls.

She rubbed her chest, certain that her heart

was going to break through. "It isn't. It can't be."

Her denial grew with each step while a knot tightened in the pit of her stomach. "It isn't. It can't be," she repeated until she finally stopped to hover over the bassinette.

For half a heartbeat, Leila relaxed. The small, perfectly formed brown baby with rosy cheeks had to be a doll, which meant someone was playing a cruel joke. However, when the angelic child cooed softly, Leila jumped back in terror.

Who would—? When did she—? Where—?

"No. No." She pivoted so fast she nearly tripped out of her pink slippers. Escaping the kitchen, she could only think to shout one name at the top of her lungs. "Sam!"

Leila bolted through the dining room and into the living room.

Both were empty.

"Sam!"

Swiveling, Leila tripped; but she saved herself from making a splat on the floor by dropping to her knees. Yet, adrenaline propelled her back to her feet and she was once again flying up and down the house.

Guest rooms—empty.

Bathrooms—empty.

Closets—empty.

"Sam…please. Don't do this to me," she begged.

Fear and anxiety knit a fine sheen of sweat across Leila's brow, but she kept going. She reached an all-time low when she crawled on all fours to check beneath her own bed.

Samantha wasn't there either.

Leila raked her fingers through her hair until her day-old mousse achieved the Bride of Frankenstein look and she nearly succumbed to the temptation to curl up into a ball. Then a thought occurred to her. She hadn't checked outside. What if Sam was still out there, trying to unload her car or something?

Granted, it was far-fetched; but hope gave credence to the wild notion. Leila sprinted down the stairs, fluffy pink slippers and all; but before she reached the front door, a thin, high-pitched wail filled the house.

Leila skidded to a stop. The baby was crying. "What should I do?"

You should go check on her.

"But I don't know how to take care of a baby."

How hard could it be?

Leila mulled over the internal question. She was a smart woman in charge of a successful publishing company. Surely she could handle a baby.

The wail climbed a few octaves and Leila was forced to head into the kitchen. "Okay, okay. I'm here," she soothed, rushing to the bassinette.

The baby stopped screaming…just long enough to draw a deep breath and then let it rip again.

With rattled eardrums, Leila panicked. She grabbed the bassinette by the handle and raced out of the house. So much for her being able to handle a baby.

"Sam!"

Garrick bolted upright, but was confused by what had awakened him. Yet, in the next second, a woman's shrill voice penetrated his double-paned windows and he was out of the bed like a shot.

"Sam!"

Widening a slit in the venetian blinds, Garrick peered out to the house across the street. This was supposed to be a quiet neighborhood.

"Sam!"

Who's Sam? His eyes lowered to the large pink basket she was carrying. A baby. Something was wrong with her baby?

Garrick turned and raced from the window. His heart lodged in his throat at all the wild possibilities. Was the baby sick, hurt, or worse?

"Sam!"

There was no snow this Christmas, but the cold December wind was an instant wake-up call against his bare chest. Yet, there was no way he was going to turn around now that he could also hear a baby screaming.

"Ma'am, ma'am. What's wrong?"

"What?" The lady stepped back. "Who are you?" Her eyes raked him.

It hit him then that he was standing in his neighbor's driveway in just his pajama pants. "I—I'm Garrick Grayson. Your new neighbor across the street."

She took another step back but confusion still

clouded her face. Actually, she looked every bit the part of a crazy woman with her hair standing straight on her head. Maybe this was trouble he didn't need.

"Ma'am, you were screaming at the top of your voice. Is something wrong?"

She blinked out of her trance and glanced around the neighborhood.

Garrick looked as well and saw a few people milling out of their houses.

"Just great," the woman mumbled under her breath. "Sam has turned me into a screaming lunatic." She turned, clutched the bassinette tighter, and headed toward her front door.

Still concerned about the crying baby, he followed. "Who's Sam?" he asked.

"My soon-to-be-deceased sister." She entered the house. "Okay, little baby," she cooed awkwardly. "You can stop crying now. Everything is going to be all right...I hope."

Garrick frowned. "Ma'am. Is everything all right? Do you need me to call someone for you?"

"Call someone. That's a good idea. I can call someone to come and help me with...uh—this baby." She stopped in the foyer and then squeezed the large bassinette onto a slim table. "But who? Everyone is gone for the holidays."

The baby wailed at full volume.

"Okay. Okay. I can do this," she affirmed and reached for the baby.

Garrick still didn't know what to make of any of this.

The baby, dressed in all pink, flailed tiny hands and feet as the screaming continued.

Dumbfounded, Garrick eyed the bizarre woman as she held the child away from her body as if the child were a stick of dynamite. "Have you ever held a baby before?"

"Uh, yeah—but never when one was crying like this. I think something is wrong with it."

It? "I take it this is not your child?"

"Good heavens, no." Her face twisted. "It's okay. It's okay," she assured the child.

Garrick wasn't too sure about that and apparently neither was the baby—if the screaming was any indication.

"Why won't it stop crying?" the lady asked in obvious distress.

It *again.* "First, I'm guessing by all the pink

that it's a girl," he said, unable to keep the sarcasm out of his voice. "Second, I'm thinking you would want to hold her a little closer to your body if you're trying to comfort her."

The lady looked as if he'd told her to jump off a cliff; but in the next second, she was bobbing her head in agreement. "Okay, okay. I can do that."

She nearly did, too—until an unmistakable sound alerted them that the baby had just unloaded half her body weight into her diaper.

"Oh-my-God," the woman croaked, stretching her arms farther out from her body. "Did you hear that?"

The corners of Garrick's lips twitched into a smile. "Yeah, I heard." He reached for the baby. This wasn't exactly the kind of emergency he'd had in mind when he'd bolted over here, but it was a job that still needed to be done.

Garrick nestled the little girl in the crook of his arm. As he swayed back and forth, the baby quieted down. "That's a good girl," he cooed, smiling down at the chubby-cheeked baby. She was actually adorable with her nest of curly hair and sweet brown eyes. Still, he couldn't imagine who was insane enough to leave their baby with this woman.

"How did you do that?" his neighbor asked, wide-eyed and open-mouthed.

"I've been told I'm a natural with babies and animals," he boasted proudly.

"You're a godsend."

The woman raked her fingers through her hair—something she should stop doing, he noted.

"Yeah, well, I guess if you just get us a new diaper, I can help you change her and get out of your hair." He didn't mean to mention her hair, but it had a way of drawing the eye.

She blinked. "A diaper?"

"You do have diapers, right?"

"Uh." She turned back toward the bassinette and searched inside it, but the only thing she pulled out was a thin envelope.

"What's that?" he asked.

"It's from Sam," she said with a note of dread, and then lifted her large, sad brown eyes up at him. "It could only mean bad news."

Chapter 3

On the porch of her Sea Symphony Villa, Roslyn stared out at Barbados's powdery white sand, turquoise sea, cerulean sky and wanted to pinch herself. Everything was postcard perfect—and yet she couldn't stop her mind from wandering back home.

"Whatcha thinking about?" Patrick eased his arms around her waist and nibbled on her exposed shoulder.

Though his lips were pleasure, they failed to draw Roslyn from her troubled thoughts. "I was thinking about Samantha," she answered honestly.

Her husband groaned and laid his head against her shoulder. "This is supposed to be our vacation."

"It is." Roslyn turned in his arms and fluttered a smile at him. "I was just hoping everything is okay, you know? This time of year is always hard for her."

Patrick nodded, but his gaze inspected her. "This time of year is also hard on you...and Leila."

Instant tears welled in Roslyn's eyes and she lowered her gaze to stare at the span of his broad chest.

Gently, he lifted her head again so their eyes met. "All I'm saying is...you can't fix your sister. Everyone has demons to fight. Samantha is going to have to fight her own."

"It's not that easy." Roslyn pushed out of his arms and shook her head. "Samantha isn't strong. She's not like Leila—who can take a lickin' and keep on tickin'. And she's not like me." She took Patrick's hand. "I have an incredible man who I can lean on and who can pick up the pieces when I fall apart."

Patrick bowed his head.

"I know you've never cared for my baby sister."

His head jerked up again. "That's not true." He hedged as he selected his next words. "I just don't like how she emotionally blackmails you...or anyone who tries to get too close."

"And what if Ms. Friedman is right? What if she has had a baby? Do you think that she's emotionally stable to raise a child?"

"We don't know—"

"Hypothetically?"

Patrick drew a deep breath and gave the questions careful consideration. "I honestly don't know."

Roslyn nodded and returned to his arms. "Neither do I."

"Your sister abandoned her baby?" Garrick asked, mentally snapping pieces of the puzzle together.

"Looks that way." Leila ripped open the thin envelope and unfolded the enclosed letter.

"Dear Leila, I'm sorry." She stopped and closed her eyes to pray for strength.

"Is that all it says?" Garrick asked, bouncing and patting the baby's back.

Slowly, the child's wails teetered off to soft coos.

Amazed, Leila glanced up. "How are you doing that?"

"It's like I said—" he cocked his head with a disarming smile "—I'm a natural."

At that moment, the little girl released a high-pitched squeal to contradict his claim.

A smug smile curved Leila's lips.

"Any chance I can get that diaper?" he asked.

"Oh." Leila's brain kicked into gear. "I think I saw a bag in the kitchen. Hopefully there's one in there." She rushed to the kitchen and breathed a sigh of relief when she spotted an unmistakable pink diaper bag on the table. "Bingo! I found it."

She unzipped the bag and found a stockpile of tiny diapers, bottled milk, plastic toys and singing stuffed frogs.

Garrick strolled into the kitchen while making funny noises to Leila's new niece.

"She's adorable," he said, taking one of the diapers. "What's her name?"

"No clue."

"You never even met her before?"

"What can I say? Not every family is like the Huxtables," Leila huffed, and then remembered the letter she still clasped in her hand.

Her new neighbor quickly changed the subject. "Where should I change her?"

Leila lowered the letter again and glanced around. "Uh, I guess we can do it in the living room?"

"Okay." He carved out a smile. "Lead the way."

Since her house was not exactly equipped with a baby-changing station, Leila settled on him lying the baby down on the sofa. Even then, she cringed at the potential mess he could make on the furniture's expensive fabric.

"Any wipes or baby powder?"

Leila blinked as if he spoke a foreign language.

"Could you check the bag?" he asked.

"Oh, yes. Of course." Leila hid her embarrassment by pivoting and racing back to the kitchen. He had to think she was a complete idiot. In ten minutes, he'd learned that she didn't know how to hold a baby, calm a baby, or even change a baby. Yet, here she was—with a baby.

"I'll never forgive her for this," Leila mumbled under her breath as she grabbed the diaper bag. When she returned to the living room, once again, she watched him coo and blubber a bunch of gibberish. All of which her niece found entertaining.

"Here you go." She handed over the bag.

"Thanks." He quickly pulled out the items he needed. "You better pay close attention, seeing you're going to have to do this about seven to ten times a day."

Leila's eyebrows leaped up. "That much?"

"Give or take." He flashed her a dimpled smile.

Her stomach clenched and she tightened the belt on her robe before, once again, remembering the letter. She unfolded it and read. "Dear Leila. I'm sorry. I know my leaving your new six-month-old niece will be a mild inconvenience..." Leila glanced up. "A mild inconvenience?"

Garrick looked at her but said nothing.

Leila rolled her eyes and returned her attention back to the letter. "Like me, motherhood was never a part of your plans. However, unlike me, your decision wasn't based on the fact that you would make a lousy mother, but simply because you're married to your career. I, on the other hand, am a screwup. I always have been."

Leila's voice softened. "Since little Emma came into my life, I'm seized by the fear that I'm going to screw her up as well. That's the last thing I want to do. Emma deserves all the things I can't give her, but I know that you can. Please don't hate me for doing this. But I believe I'm doing what's best for my daughter. Take care of her and love her as your own. Both of you will always be in my thoughts and in my heart. Love, Sam."

Leila crumpled the letter in her hand. "Give me a break."

Garrick cast another sidelong glance in her direction.

"Trust me," she said, folding her arms. "My sister is a piece of work. Every time things get tough, she gets going."

"But there's a little girl caught in the middle," Garrick said.

"Yeah." Leila fell silent as she stared down at Emma. She could see hints of Sam in the shape of the child's face and nose.

"Well," Garrick said, folding up the used diaper. "I'm all done here. You have someplace I can put this?"

Panic seized her. "You're leaving?"

"Well. There's no real reason for me to stick around."

Emma kicked and giggled to herself.

"Besides," Garrick chuckled and smiled, "I don't think this little lady will be giving you any more trouble." He tickled the child's sides and was rewarded with another burst of giggles. "She's adorable."

"But—but. I didn't see how you did the diaper thingy," Leila said.

"Trust me." He laughed as he stood. "It's pretty self-explanatory." He tried to hand the used diaper over.

Leila turned up her nose and waved the odorous thing away. "Hold on." She turned and bolted back toward the kitchen. When she returned, she carried her large stainless-steel garbage can with her. "Drop it in here."

Garrick's brows dipped in confusion, but he did as she asked. "Um, is there anyone you can call to help you with her?" He reached down and picked up the rolling child before she fell off the sofa.

Leila shook her head and set the garbage can down.

"Another family member...or friend?"

She snapped her fingers and raced over to the cordless phone on the end table. "Ciara!"

Garrick brightened. "There you go. Problem solved."

"You're so right. Ciara totally knows about this whole baby thing. I can pawn Ms. Emma off on her for a few hours while I hunt down my mentally handicapped sister." She punched in the number.

He frowned. "Do you think that's a wise idea?"

She listened as the phone rang. "What do you mean?"

"Well, apparently your sister is, uh, a little unstable at the moment. Maybe it's not the right time to force her to take care of Emma. You know, I read an article the other day on postpartum depression—"

"What are you, a shrink?"

"No—"

"Tom Cruise?"

He chuckled. "Definitely not."

Suddenly, Ciara's voice filtered onto the line. "Hello."

"Ciara! Thank God you're home."

"You've reached the Winstons' residence. Sorry, we're not able to come to the phone right now."

"Damn it!" She slammed the phone down onto its cradle.

"Uh, there's a baby in the room." Garrick's expression twisted as he attempted to cover Emma's ears.

Leila waved him off. "She doesn't know what I'm saying."

Garrick drew a deep, patient breath. "Children are like sponges. They absorb everything."

"Uh-huh." Leila folded her arms and scrutinized him carefully. "I take it you have children?"

He shifted Emma to his other arm. "Not exactly."

Her eyebrows dipped to the center of her forehead. "It's a yes or no question."

"Then the answer is no." He walked over to her. "But I'm a highly qualified uncle—who incidentally understands the Gerber baby meal plan, knows the difference between a hungry wail and a teething wail, and I am pretty skilled in the diaper-changing arena." He tried to hand over Emma.

"Wait a minute…I don't—"

"Come on. You can do it." He slid Emma into Leila's arms and proceeded to instruct her on the proper way to hold the child. "There. You already have the hang of it." He turned and exited out of the living room.

"Wait. Where are you going?"

"Home." He strode across the foyer.

"But you can't go," she reasoned, giving chase.

He laughed, but refused to stop. "Why can't I?"

"Because I *need* you." She reached out and grabbed him by the arm. "I don't know anything about babies. What if— What if I—?"

"What if you what?" Garrick turned and glanced back at her.

Leila's mind went blank. "I don't know. What

if I break her…or scar her for life or something? That happens a lot in my family."

When he chuckled, she snatched back her hand and struggled to extinguish a spark of anger.

He sensed he'd offended her and turned toward her with another breathtaking smile. "You're going to be fine," he reassured. "Women have been taking care of babies since Adam and Eve. That's what they were put on this earth for. It's in your nature."

"What?"

"It's in your nature," he repeated.

Leila stared at him. "What kind of sexist pig are you?"

Garrick blinked. "Excuse me?"

"It's in our nature?" She stepped back. "Is that the best you can do? I'm standing here telling you that I could potentially emotionally scar a little girl and your response is a flippant 'It's in my nature'?"

"Well—"

"You know. Never mind." She marched over to the door and held it open. "Thanks for your *so-called* help."

He stared at her; but when she lifted her head and refused to meet his gaze again, he shrugged and strolled toward the door. When he reached it, he stopped and contemplated whether he needed to apologize; but there was something about the firm line of her jaw and the height of her nose that made him reconsider.

"Merry Christmas," he said, and walked out.

The door slammed as soon as he crossed the threshold. Garrick looked back and shook his head. "At least Scrooge was sane."

Chapter 4

Samantha Owens sobbed behind the wheel of her fifteen-year-old beat-up sedan. Her guilt weighed down her shoulders while the hole in her heart expanded. It had been nearly thirty minutes since she'd left Emma at her sister's house—the longest thirty minutes of her life.

"You did the right thing," the devil on her shoulder repeated—or was it the angel? She was so mixed up, she couldn't tell them apart anymore. Frustrated, she dropped her head against the center of the steering wheel, and then jumped when the horn blared.

She sat up and glanced around Leila's quiet neighborhood. Leila's front door jerked open and for a moment, Samantha feared the worst. Instead, a handsome stranger emerged and then jumped when the front door slammed behind him.

A classic Leila move.

However, the neighbor seemed more amused than angry as he strolled with a confident swagger across the street. He was quite a specimen and she wondered whether he and her sister were more than just neighbors.

Sam dispelled the notion and refocused her attention on Leila's McMansion. "I did the right thing," she concluded, starting the car. "Bye, Emma. Mommy loves you."

Garrick returned home and made a beeline to the kitchen for a pot of coffee; but after a morning with the unforgettable Leila Owens, maybe he needed something with a little more kick.

"Was a simple 'thank you' too much to ask

for?" He shook his head and reached for his favorite can of Santo Domingo coffee. "Come to think of it, she probably never said the words before.

"She'll need me again," he assured himself. "Undoubtedly needing help warming a baby's bottle. Career women." He shook his head.

The doorbell rang.

He stopped and turned with a smug smile. "Surprise, surprise," he mumbled as he donned a sweatshirt. He headed toward the front door and opened it with a flourish. "And what can I do for you now, Leila?"

"Merry Christmas!" Orlando and his family shouted at him with armloads of wrapped gifts.

Startled, Garrick jerked back in surprise. "Oh, uh, Merry Christmas to you, too. Uh, come on in." He stepped back and watched them enter one by one.

"Uncle Garrick, were you surprised?" his three-year-old niece, Omara, asked.

Garrick knelt down to her level. "I sure was, honey. I can't believe you were able to keep a secret from me. It must have been hard."

"Real hard." Omara blinked her long, black,

curly lashes and slid her arms around his neck. "I got a 'nother surprise for you."

"You do?" He gathered her into his arms and stood. "What kind of surprise?" He closed the door.

"I gotcha a present."

"Oh?" Garrick rounded his eyes as wide as he could get them. "I looovve presents."

Omara giggled.

"Uh, who is Leila?" Tamara asked, sliding out of her coat.

"What?"

Tamara glanced at her husband. "Isn't that what he said when he answered the door?"

Orlando shrugged. "I didn't catch the name."

"Well, I did." She walked over to her brother-in-law and met his gaze with her hands firmly jammed onto her hips. "Who is she? And think twice before lying to me. You know I have my ways of finding the truth."

Garrick chuckled at Tamara aka the human lie detector. "Calm down. It's not what you think."

"You don't know what I'm thinking."

"You don't," Orlando piped in. "Nobody does. Nobody wants to know."

Tamara turned her narrowed eyes toward him.

"Just trying to help my brother out." He shrugged and returned his gaze to Garrick. "You're on your own, bro."

"I just want to make sure there isn't another woman in the picture before I send him out on a date with one of my best friends. That's all."

"Then you can relax." Garrick led them out of the foyer and toward the living room. "Leila is just my crazy neighbor across the street."

Tamara perked. "You've already met your neighbors?"

"Just the one…and I'm already regretting it."

Leila was ready to pull her hair out by the roots. Who knew something so tiny could be so loud…for so long? "Give me a few more minutes and your bottle will be ready," she reassured.

She practiced bouncing the baby and patting her back the same way Garrick had, but it wasn't working. Neither were her sorry attempts to warm up a freakin' bottle. She'd warmed one up in the microwave with disastrous results, and she quickly learned leaving a bottle to heat for more than ten minutes on the stove caused the milky stuff to separate from the watery stuff.

Now she was on the quest to discover the perfect time for a baby bottle to warm. Meanwhile, Emma hollered as though she hadn't eaten since Philip had passed the bread at the last supper.

"Okay. Okay, Emma," she cooed. "I think this is going to be it." Leila removed the bottle. "So far so good."

Belatedly, she remembered seeing Roslyn test a bottle by squirting milk onto the back of her hand to double check the temperature, and she followed suit. However, the top wasn't screwed on tight enough and it popped off the moment she turned the bottle over on her hand.

"Damn it!" She jumped back and managed *not* to drop the baby.

Emma screamed and nearly pierced Leila's eardrum.

"What? Why are *you* screaming? I'm the one scalded."

Her niece didn't seem to care as she sucked more oxygen into her lungs and let it rip a second time.

Tears welled in the back of Leila's eyes as her

frustration reached an all-time high. She simply wasn't made out for this sort of thing, but what choice did she have but to trudge through it?

"Okay. Okay. Please stop crying. Auntie Leila is doing the best she can." She bounced and patted her some more as she made her way back to the diaper bag. "I'm sure we have another bottle in the bag."

She was wrong.

"Oh, no. No. No." She searched every inch of the bag at least ten times. "Please, God. Say this isn't happening."

But it was.

"Okay. I have to think." However, Emma's screams made it impossible.

Maybe her next-door neighbor…

Leila shook the rogue thought from her head. She couldn't go back over there after the way she'd behaved—and she'd behaved badly. She still held in her defense that she'd practically begged the man for help, but he'd been so damn determined to bolt out of there that she… Okay, so there was really no excuse for her behavior.

Exhaling, Leila dug back through the bag

and found small glass jars of baby food. "Oh, thank God." She exhaled. "Let's see what we have in here." She returned to the stove, but once again was plagued with how long it took to warm up food.

Her stomach rumbled and reminded her that she, too, needed breakfast. "One thing at a time," she told herself. "Okay, we have some very interesting-looking chicken and beef here."

Emma bucked in her arms and grabbed a healthy portion of Leila's hair.

"Ouch, you little spoiled brat." Leila dropped one of the glass jars and ignored it when it shattered at her feet. "Let go." She tugged for Emma to release her hold. Instead, the child yanked harder and intensified Leila's mountainous headache. With one last pull, she finally let go.

"Oh, I give up." Leila spun around and marched out of the kitchen. "Pride be damned. I can't do this."

Now dressed in a comfortable pair of jeans and a T-shirt, Garrick returned to the sparsely decorated living room with a six-inch tabletop

Christmas tree that easily made Charlie Brown's worthy for Times Square.

As he entered, Omara shrieked with joy at the sight of the armload of gifts he'd purchased.

Tamara rolled her eyes and shook her head. "We'd agreed on just one gift."

"You *said* one gift, but I never agreed to it," he reminded her with a soft smile and set the gifts down in the center of the floor.

His niece squealed in delight as she flew from her father's lap to the packages.

"You two do nothing but spoil her," Tamara complained.

Garrick laughed. "That's what you're supposed to do with little girls."

"She knows," Orlando said, winking at his wife. "She's nothing but a big daddy's girl herself." He returned his attention to his brother. "Every time I see her father, he's cleaning his gun."

"I don't blame him. She could've done better."

Orlando's brows dipped. "Hey!"

"What?" Garrick jabbed a thumb at his chest. "I was available."

"You stay away from my wife, bro." Orlando looped an arm around her waist. "I mean it. You play too much."

"Daddy, look!" Omara tottered over to showcase her latest baby doll. "It cries just like a real baby!"

"Oh, joy." Orlando smote his brother with a narrowed gaze.

"Hey, anything for the kids." Garrick chuckled.

"That's all right," Tamara said, patting her husband's leg. "Revenge will be ours when he finally has children."

"If he can convince a woman to reproduce."

Garrick's smile disappeared. "That's a low blow, man."

"Cheer up. You were a hot commodity back in college. You just need to dust off your old player skills and jump back into the game."

"Thanks for the pointers."

"Anytime."

The doorbell rang.

Garrick stood and headed for the door. "But Tamara's right. I'll have my turn one day. Hopefully sooner than later."

Orlando and Tamara glanced at each other with knowing smiles.

"Is there something you want to tell us, bro?" Orlando shouted after him. "Do you have a bun in the oven somewhere?"

Garrick opened the door and then jumped back as a hysterical Leila breezed through.

"I can't do this! I can't do this!" She thrust Emma into his arms. "Here. If this is a woman thing, I'm missing a few genes."

"What—?"

"I can't fix a bottle…. I can't even warm a jar of food—a damn jar."

Garrick turned the child away from her. "We've been over this. Watch your language!" He stroked the child's back and she immediately quieted down.

Leila's eyes narrowed as she jabbed a finger into his chest. "Since you know so much, you take care of her."

A stunned Tamara and Orlando inched into the foyer.

"Bro?"

Tamara folded her arms. "Aren't you going to introduce us?"

Garrick turned and then followed their wide stares. "Oh, no. She's not... We're not... This isn't what it looks like."

Chapter 5

Leila felt like an ass.

"You have company," she said, pointing out the obvious and backing toward the door. "I—I'm sorry." She reached for Emma while a tidal wave of embarrassment crashed within her.

Garrick stepped back as his eyebrows rose in surprise and in amusement. "Apology accepted." He faced his family again. "I'll be right back."

Tamara's eyes darted between her brother-in-law and Leila. "Is there something wrong?"

"No, no." Garrick gestured Leila toward the door. "This will only take a moment. Just tell Omara I'll be right back." He followed his neighbor across the threshold and closed the door behind them.

Once alone on the front porch, Leila slumped against the white colonial column. "This day couldn't possibly get any worse."

"I take it you weren't able to find anyone to help you?"

"It's Christmas. Everyone I know is out of town or just cruelly avoiding my phone calls," she complained, warding off tears. After a long, sidelong glance, she couldn't discern if he thought she was a raving lunatic or not. Then again, why wouldn't he?

"Look, about earlier—"

"Forget about it." He smiled and glanced down at the sleeping baby nestled against his chest. "Looks like your little angel is knocked out."

"Angel? Try devil." Leila chuckled. "She hasn't stopped screaming since you left."

"Ah, poor thing," he said as he descended the front stairs.

Leila's gaze followed and took note of his strong shoulders, broad back and his cute butt. "Not bad," she mumbled.

Garrick glanced back over his shoulder. "Are you coming?"

She blinked. "Oh. Yes, I'm right behind you."

Tamara and Orlando crowded together at the window by the front door. "What do you think is going on?" Tamara whispered.

"I have no idea, but did you see her hair?"

"Her hair?" Tamara leaned back to stare at her husband. "Surely that wasn't the only thing you noticed?"

"Oh, you mean the baby?"

"Duh." She popped him on the back of the head.

"What's going on?" Omara joined them at the window, hugging two more dolls. "Where's Uncle Garrick?"

Orlando peeked out the blinds again. "He, uh, just went to help out a neighbor. He'll be right back."

"Will I get to play with *his* baby when he comes back?"

Orlando glanced over at his wife's smug smile. "Out of the mouths of babes."

Now that her moment of temporary insanity had come to an end, Leila stepped out of the shower refreshed. Maybe it was all she needed to get a firm grip on her new situation. She donned her gray sweat suit and ran a brush through her hair while she blow-dried it straight. Minutes later, she descended the stairs.

"Wow. You clean up well," Garrick complimented.

Flattered by the unexpected praise, Leila smiled as she stopped in front of him. "Where's Emma?"

"Napping." He smiled back and shoved his hands into his pants pockets. "I, uh, cleaned up the mess in the kitchen, made a bottle, and jotted some notes on how to warm up everything."

A blanket of shame covered Leila. "Look, my behavior today is inexcusable."

"There's no need—"

"Please, let me finish." Her lips slid wider as she gazed up at him, noticing his brown eyes were more like the color of Hershey's Kisses. "I'm normally a sane person and I truly appreciate you for not calling a mental institution to come and pick me up. You've gone beyond the call of duty for a new neighbor." She shrugged. "Thank you."

Garrick waited, and then asked, "Is that it?"

"If there's anything I can do for you, please don't hesitate to ask."

He chuckled. "You don't owe me anything," he assured and turned toward the door. "I was happy to help. If there's something I forgot to write down, I'm just across the street."

Though his words were kind, Leila couldn't help but feel a chill—a distance.

Garrick stopped at the door. "If you need anything else—"

"I won't. I mean—I've bothered you enough. I even dragged you away from your family...on Christmas," she added with a small laugh.

He forced out a chuckle and shuffled out the door.

She watched him leave, still feeling like a complete ass.

* * *

"That poor woman," Tamara exclaimed after Garrick relayed this morning's shenanigans with his new neighbor. "Can you imagine waking up to something like that?" she asked her husband.

"I highly doubt you would run out in the neighborhood screaming like a banshee," Garrick said, admiring his new watch from his niece.

"Don't be so sure." She rolled her eyes and shook her head. "A baby is a big deal—a lot of work, a life-changing event."

Garrick and Orlando frowned.

"I'm just saying, I probably would've freaked, too."

"But you already have a kid," he reasoned.

Tamara's eyes widened as her nose flared. "So what?" she snapped. "Sleep deprivation, constant feedings, and an endless assembly line of diaper changes are not my idea of fun."

Orlando looked stunned. "I thought we were going to try for a boy?"

"Not right now," she said, folding her arms. "I want to go back to school and start my own business."

"You want to become a career woman?" Garrick said, unable to keep the disappointment out of his voice. "Why would you want to do that?"

"Can't you conquer the world *after* I have my son?" Orlando added.

Tamara ignored her husband and turned her attention back to Garrick. "And what's wrong with a woman wanting a career? This is the twenty-first century. We don't all want to be barefoot and pregnant or devote our entire lives to being housewives. At least I don't."

"I'm not saying you should," Garrick defended. "I just think—"

"Ah." Tamara set down her glass of Coke and pointed a finger at Garrick. "I know what this is about."

"No. No." Garrick quickly held up his hands and shook his head.

"Yes. Yes. This is about Miranda," Tamara accused, and then rocked back with a hearty laugh. "That's why you want to steer away from career women."

Garrick and Orlando looked guiltily at each other.

"I don't have a problem with career women," he denied. At Tamara's dubious stare, he added, "I just don't want to marry another one."

"Uh-huh." Tamara crossed her arms. "Your neighbor is right. You *are* a sexist pig."

"What?" Garrick glanced at his brother for help, but saw Orlando looking around as if he didn't want any part of the conversation. "Okay, yes. There were some lessons learned from my marriage. The main one—I want a family, and people who want families should not marry those who don't."

"Women can have a career and a family."

Garrick laughed. "That's a myth."

"What?"

He looked to his brother again.

"You're on your own, bro," Orlando laughed. "I live with her."

Tamara smote her husband with a look and he quickly fell silent again.

"Fine. I'll go it alone." Garrick met Tamara's gaze. "I don't know who sold women on the idea they could have it all, but it's not true. It's impossible to run a business and a household harmoniously and successfully. Something has to give and Leila Owens is going to learn that *real* soon."

"Okay, little Emma." Leila drew a deep breath and slipped on a pair of yellow rubber gloves. "Let's change your diaper."

Emma squirmed on the sofa and rewarded her aunt with a gummy smile.

Leila's heart squeezed and she grudgingly smiled back. However, her lips curled the other direction the moment she peeled back the diaper. "Good Lord, what was in that bottle?"

Emma giggled and kicked her legs.

"Oh, child. Please don't do that." She tried to catch the baby's legs; but she wasn't successful until after Emma had made a bigger mess. Success came after a half box of baby wipes and a mushroom cloud of baby powder. Other than that— "Perfect!"

Leila lifted Emma and then watched in dismay as her creation slid off the child's heinie. Of course, her niece chose that moment to pee all over her white sofa.

"Goddamn it, Sam."

Chapter 6

The first workday after Christmas, *Atlanta Spice* returned to its usual buzz of hectic calm where photographers were late, freelance writers were behind schedule, and the company's CEO was still recovering from a mental breakdown.

"She's adorable," Ciara cooed, waving the stuffed frog in front of a giggling Emma. "How could you not love a face like this?" She leaned over and planted a kiss against the baby's chubby cheeks.

"She's only adorable in front of company, but not when she's peeing on my couch." Leila looked up from her desk. "Which cost me a pretty penny to have cleaned. Not to mention the cost of turning one of the guest rooms into a nursery."

"You already hired someone to do that?"

"Had to. I'm not going to keep changing Ms. Thang on my expensive furniture. I'm paying a decorator double time to have the room done by the end of the day."

Ciara continued to coo over the child. "Have you had any luck locating Sam?"

"None." Leila removed her reading glasses and leaned back in her oversize office chair. "It's like she disappeared off the face of the earth. Which might be a wise move on her part because if I ever get my hands on her—"

"A woman who can just walk away from her child has to be in a lot of pain," Ciara sympathized. "That's the only explanation I can come up with."

Leila didn't respond, but sat up and returned her attention to the stacks of paper on her desk.

"Of course, you look like hell."

"I haven't slept for more than two hours since

Christmas Eve," Leila complained, staring at her niece. "I don't know how anybody does it. I feel like a walking zombie."

"When is Roslyn returning from her vacation?"

"Five days."

"Are you going to make it?"

"I'm a survivor." Leila straightened in her chair. "I've had to get through a lot worse."

"You're going to hire a nanny, aren't you?"

"Damn right." Leila glanced at her watch. "I have an important meeting tonight and I have no intentions of dragging a screaming baby into a five-star restaurant. Hearst Communications has the distribution that can take this magazine to the next level. I simply can't miss or reschedule this meeting."

"What about that gorgeous hunk across the street from you?" Ciara smiled.

Leila regretted telling Ciara that part of the story. "*Gorgeous* doesn't do him justice." Dropping her elbows down on her desk, she sighed and indulged in a moment to reflect on the best butt she'd seen on a man.

"You know, it's not every day a woman runs into a baby whisperer."

She snapped out of her trance. "Okay. Now you're just making this stuff up."

"C'mon. You know what I mean. A man who can change diapers, fix bottles and rock a baby to sleep…?" She sobered. "Are you sure he's not married?"

"I didn't see a ring." Leila shrugged as she gave the question considerable thought. "I don't think so."

"Did he show up on your gaydar?"

"Not even a bleep."

"Well." Ciara clapped her hands. "I say we jump his bones."

"We?" Leila laughed.

"I'm a pregnant married woman. I have to live vicariously through someone. It might as well be you."

"What? *Elmo* isn't getting it for you?"

"Lay off my husband's name," Ciara warned. "I think it's cute."

Emma cooed and giggled at the playpen's rotating mobile.

The women glanced over at the child and smiled.

"Are you sure you want to pawn her off on some stranger?"

"Look, I have a company to run." Leila perked. "Unless you and Elmo—"

"I would if I could, but Elmo's parents are flying in tonight." Ciara patted her belly. "We told them the news on Christmas morning and now they insist on coming in for a visit. But I think you're missing a wonderful opportunity to peek inside what motherhood is like."

"My view of motherhood has not changed. It's not for me."

"Still. You know you have to be very careful whom you leave a child with. In fact, it's not unheard of to run a criminal and credit check, and then you might want to set up cameras throughout the house so you can keep an eye out on what's going on."

Leila hadn't considered all of that; but now, since Ciara had brought it up, one could never be too careful.

Once Ciara returned to her desk, Leila spent the next twenty minutes feeding, burping and obsessing with whether she made the right decision to hire a nanny. It suddenly seemed risky.

"Ms. Owens, your one o'clock appointment is here to see you," Ciara reported over the speakerphone.

"Send her in."

The moment the door opened, Emma started crying. No wonder, given the middle-aged Englishwoman's frosty nature.

"You have an impressive résumé, Ms. Howard." Leila smiled and tried Garrick's patting-and-bouncing trick.

"Children are my life," Ms. Howard said without smiling. "All they need is a strict set of rules and a firm hand."

Leila shifted and wondered at her meaning.

"Holding the child like that is just spoiling her." The woman's thin lips pursed as she shook her head. "It's not good to reward bad behavior."

"Excuse me?" Leila shouted above Emma's wails.

The elderly woman stood from her chair and reached for the baby. "May I see her?"

Emma clutched Leila's blouse and screamed louder. Did her niece sense something strange about the woman?

You know you have to be very careful whom you leave a child with.

"Uh, no." Leila turned away from the experienced nanny. "I think that's enough with the questions for the day." She yelled above the wails and flashed a tight smile. "I'll be in contact."

Ms. Howard drew her hands back and stared down the end of her nose. "Very well." She gathered her things. "I hope to hear from you."

As soon as the door closed behind the Englishwoman, Emma stopped crying.

Leila frowned at her sniffling, wide-eyed niece and wondered what the devil had just happened. "You know, I'm starting to think you're like your mother—high-maintenance."

Emma batted her long lashes, flashed her dimpled cheeks and released a high giggle.

"Whatever."

Interview after interview, Emma screamed, kicked or threw up on her potential nannies. At the end of the day, Leila felt as if she hadn't accomplished anything. Her in-box overflowed with work. Her designer suit was stained with drool, food and only God knew what else. "And I still don't have a babysitter."

* * *

Garrick spent the day unpacking what seemed like an endless line of boxes. By the time the sun set, he was convinced he'd barely scratched the surface. Maybe Tamara was right and he needed to hire someone to do this. One thing was certain—he needed a decorator. In the divorce, Miranda had made off with the good furniture, plants and pictures.

The only things left were nondescript items that left his new house bland and cold. He glanced around and struggled to ward off a wave of nostalgia. "So much for a new beginning."

He meandered over to the refrigerator and opened it for the millionth time. A lone pack of hot dogs, two cans of beer, and a half a bottle of Gatorade stared back at him. Maybe if he left now, he could make it to his brother's in time for dinner.

Tamara could throw down in the kitchen.

The doorbell rang.

Garrick jerked up his head and frowned. He wasn't expecting anyone. He closed the fridge, headed toward the front door and peeked out the peephole.

On the other side, Leila stood in a white sequined dress bouncing little Emma on her hip.

"Oh, Lord," he mumbled, lowering his head against the door.

When the doorbell rang again, he pulled himself together and answered it.

"Ms. Owens." He slid his lips wider than necessary. "What a nice surprise."

"Hi, Mr. Grayson." She smiled nervously. "I hope I'm not interrupting anything?"

"Uh, no. I was just…peddling around." His gaze landed on Emma's bright eyes and chubby cheeks, and his smile turned genuine. "Is there a problem?"

"Well, yes…and no."

Garrick's gaze swung back to hers. He took special note of how her upswept hair made her look younger—softer. "So, are you going to tell me what's up or are we going to play twenty questions?"

At his light reprimand, Leila squared her shoulders, but still looked vulnerable.

"Would you like to come in?" he softened his tone.

"Actually, I just came over to see…well,

really I needed to ask a favor. But, never mind. It was a stupid idea." She turned to leave and Emma screwed up her face.

"I take it you need a babysitter?" Garrick asked, crossing his arms and admiring the rear view. She really could fill out a dress.

Leila stopped, but refused to turn around. "I—I know it's short notice and I don't want to inconvenience you—"

"But you need a babysitter?"

She stood mute while she warred with her pride. What was it about the man that got under her skin?

Garrick, on the other hand, found the exchange amusing. "But I guess I'm wrong." He shrugged and turned away from the door.

"It would just be for a couple of hours." She turned, unable to keep the pleading from her eyes.

"Then you're in luck." He winked at Emma. "I just happen to have a few hours to kill."

Leila sighed in relief. "How long were you going to make me sweat?"

"What are you talking about?" He laughed. "I threw you a hook the moment you turned those lost-puppy-dog eyes on me." He leaned forward and reached out for Emma. "That's a very old trick, by the way."

To Leila's surprise, her niece also reached for Garrick. "I guess you really are a natural."

"I told you." He grabbed his keys from a hook near the door and stepped out of the house. "So what's the special occasion?" he asked as he locked up.

"Business dinner." She straightened her shoulders. "A very important night for my magazine."

He should have known. He let her lead the way back across the street and admired the view all the way. How come someone like her didn't have a man around?

"I should be home no later than ten—ten-thirty tops," she said, entering through the front door. "Bottles are in the fridge. There is a changing station in both the living room and the first guest room on your right upstairs—"

"Oh?" He looked at her, again impressed with her progress. "You're getting the hang of this."

"I don't have a choice." She grabbed a full-length faux-fur coat from the closet next to the door. "There's plenty of food in the kitchen, you're welcome to help yourself. My cell-phone number is taped on the fridge. Please call me if you need something or if you have an emergency. Of course, you're probably more equipped to handle it than I, but call me anyway. Uh, let's see, am I forgetting something?"

"I think we're going to be fine." He bounced Emma on his arm. "Isn't that right, Emma?"

The baby wrinkled her nose and gave him a big toothless grin.

"She really likes you."

"Hey, I'm—"

"Yeah, yeah. You're a natural. Well, let me tell you something, Mr. Garrick Grayson son of Robert and Patricia Grayson, brother to Orlando Grayson of 555 Johnson Ferry Road in Alpharetta, Georgia. If you harm one strand of hair on my niece's head, I'll hunt you down and kill you. Are we clear?"

He blinked. "What are you—a federal agent?"

Leila winked. "See you at ten-thirty." She kissed Emma on the cheek and waved as she slipped out the door.

Garrick smiled at the closed door. "There just might be hope for you yet, Leila Owens."

Chapter 7

Garrick was in love.

Not since Omara had come into the world had another baby captured his heart and wrapped him around her finger. It wasn't because Emma dug his sock-puppet act or the way he flew her around the living room like an airplane, either. Quite simply: it was her laugh.

She was beyond adorable when she rocked her head back and gave a full belly laugh. After a couple hours, he found himself longing for a family again.

Yet, the prospect of jumping back in the dating arena and starting from scratch made him exhausted just thinking about it.

"Maybe I should just resign myself to being the best uncle in the world." He tweaked Emma's nose. "What do you think?"

Emma gurgled and mumbled nonsensical words.

"You know, I wouldn't mind if you called me Uncle Garrick," he admitted. "But I can understand your hesitation, seeing how we just met and all."

Another belly laugh accompanied a drooling kiss against his cheek.

"I have you pegged now," he laughed, wiping the side of his face. "You're going to drive all the boys crazy, aren't you?"

Emma's head dropped forward.

"I'm going to take that as a *yes.*" He winked and then waved a finger. "You have to make me a promise. When you grow up to be all beautiful and everything, you have to take it easy on simple boys like me."

He smiled and wondered about what life had in store for the little beauty. Had her mother truly run off or would she come back once guilt weighed her down?

"Well, I think your aunt is going to take good care of you. I don't have anything to base that on," he admitted. "But you have to admit, she's doing a heck of a lot better than that first day you arrived."

Emma nodded and grabbed his finger in an attempt to pull it into her mouth.

Garrick reached for her bottle of apple juice, nestled her on his lap, and made himself comfortable in an armchair. She lifted her large brown eyes at him as she drank from her bottle.

"You know, you have eyes like your aunt," he noted. "Has anyone ever told you that? Probably not, seeing how you two also just met." He chuckled at his joke.

A silver-framed photograph caught Garrick's attention. In the picture, Leila stood smiling in between two women with equally broad and similar smiles. Each was attractive, but it was Leila who commanded his full attention.

Her eyes and smile hinted and teased him as if she knew a secret. A genuine love radiated between the women and he wondered if one of the other ladies was Emma's mother. Still, his gaze returned to Leila.

If a picture was worth a thousand words, what did this one say about his neighbor? *Sexy* leaped to mind, and another image of her in her white evening dress surfaced. She was a woman who owned her curves and, to be honest, he wouldn't mind roaming his hands down—

Emma coughed.

Garrick quickly cleaned his thoughts. "What? I wasn't doing anything."

She said nothing, but he imagined she didn't believe him.

"Okay. So I was thinking about your aunt," he confessed. "Generally speaking, she's pretty hot. However, it would never work between us."

Emma's eyes drooped low.

"I don't really expect you to understand. Things really get complicated when you get older. Physical attraction isn't enough." His gaze crept back to the picture. "Things like compatibility are important. You know, finding someone who has the same hopes, dreams, and ideas."

The soft suckling of air caught his attention

and he glanced down to see Emma's bottle empty, and she had fallen fast asleep.

"Yeah, my love life bores me, too."

Leila couldn't concentrate.

Every time Mr. Porter, her business date, rambled on about projects, distribution, or even how overcooked his steak was, Leila kept contemplating to call home. Sure, she'd run a few reports on her new neighbor, but how responsible was it to leave her niece with a man she hardly knew?

"I have to admit—I'm impressed with how far you've taken *Atlanta Spice* in such a short time," Porter said. "You've been in business— what—five years?" He cocked his head as his gray eyes leveled on her. "Ms. Owens?"

"Huh? Oh. Uh, six. I started *Atlanta Spice* six years ago." She broadened her plastic smile. "I truly believe the magazine and Hearst Communications will make an excellent partnership."

Porter dropped his gaze and his jiggling, thick neck reddened as he drew a deep breath.

She frowned as her antennae rose. "Is something wrong?"

"No." He cleared his throat and carved on a new smile. "You are a very smart business-woman and we at Hearst admire what you've accomplished in an oversaturated market."

Leila lifted her chin as a swell of accomplishment grew within her.

"But—" He lowered his gaze again. "Hearst doesn't share the same vision for the magazine."

Confused, Leila stared at him. Mentally, she pictured an airplane plummeting to the ground. "I don't understand."

Porter lowered his fork and then braided his fingers above his plate. "We're interested in *purchasing Atlanta Spice.*" He let his words set in for a moment before he continued, "We're prepared to offer you a fair price for the magazine. Trust me. You'll never have to work again."

"It's not for sale," Leila managed to say.

"Everything is for sale," he retaliated. "It's just simply finding the right price." He held her gaze. "Look, Ms. Owens. You've taken this magazine as far as it can go. There's no shame in cashing in a cash cow and moving on to the next big adventure. A beautiful woman like yourself, surely there's some man you have tucked in a corner?"

Uncertain about the direction the conversation was headed, Leila removed her emotions from her expression.

"I know when my wife was about your age she kept screaming about her biological clock."

His sentence hung in the air between them while Leila envisioned knocking his smug smile off his face. Why did men think *all* women wanted babies?

"I appreciate your concern over my biological clock, but let's focus, shall we?"

Porter shifted and had the nerve to look indignant.

"I'm looking for a new distribution deal," she began, battling to remain calm. "If I can't get it with you then regretfully I'll have to get it somewhere else."

Porter didn't bat an eye when he leaned forward. "Why don't you at least hear our offer before you make a decision?"

It was close to midnight when a depressed Leila returned home. She'd left the restaurant hours ago but had ended up taking an uncharted drive around Atlanta's perimeter.

No matter what she did, she couldn't get Hearst's offer out of her head. Whenever she felt tempted to accept it, she was crushed with disappointment. How could she ever give up her baby?

Her thoughts leaped to Samantha and she lowered her head against the steering wheel. After a while, she cut the engine and wondered if she had angered her neighbor by returning so late. As she stepped out of the car and approached the front door, she wondered about the going rate for babysitters.

Entering the house, she thanked God for the welcoming silence; yet, as she slipped out of her coat, she grew concerned about it.

"Hello?" she called out as she closed the coat closet.

When she didn't receive an answer, she inched toward the living room. "Garrick, where are you?"

Something rustled on the sofa and Leila tiptoed and approached from the back. Once she stood above it, she gazed down at the most angelic sight she'd ever seen.

A sleeping Garrick lay flat on his back while

Emma dozed softly on his chest. Since both seemed cozy and content, she didn't have the heart to wake either of them.

Still, the sight of them awakened something foreign in her and she stared at them while it grew until she recognized the feeling as longing.

Garrick sighed and then slowly his eyes fluttered open. "Hey," he greeted.

"Hey, yourself," she whispered back. "Sorry I'm late."

An easy smile curled Garrick's lips. "Not a problem. I rather enjoyed it."

Leila continued smiling, but shook her head. "How is it that someone who loves children as much as you doesn't have any of his own?"

His smile shaved a few inches as he glanced down at little Emma. "Just unlucky, I suppose."

"Good thing I have small feet," she sighed. "It appears I've put both of them in my mouth. Sorry."

Garrick laughed and Emma squirmed fitfully. "I better put her to bed."

"Here, let me." Leila reached down and pried the baby from him. As she laid Emma against her shoulder, that strange fluttering returned to her stomach. There was something in the way

Emma felt in her arms—something about the way her breath drifted across her skin.

"You've fallen in love with her, too," Garrick accused, sitting up.

"It's hard not to," she admitted and turned to take the child upstairs. As Leila walked, she hummed nursery rhymes she was surprised she remembered. When she tucked her niece into bed, she stalled to watch her sleep.

Leila thought about her own mother for the first time in years. Had her mom ever watched her daughters while they'd slept? Had she had dreams and hopes for their future—or had she only thought of herself, the way she had when she'd taken her life?

"I better get going," Garrick whispered from the doorway.

Leila jumped and then crept out of the room. "Sorry." She pulled the door up. "I just…I don't know."

"Where did you go?"

"I was just thinking about someone." She flashed a smile.

"Oh." Garrick held up his hands. "I didn't mean to pry."

"No. It's okay." She shook her head and pretended that she didn't feel the squeeze to her heart. "It wasn't anyone important."

Garrick nodded, but he didn't look as though he believed her. Great, the last thing she needed was a man who could read her like an open book.

"Um…excuse me if this is tacky, but how much do I owe you for this evening?"

He shrugged. "Well, I'm pretty expensive," he warned. "I make about three, four hundred dollars an hour on my day job." He glanced at his watch. "You've been gone for about five hours. That will be two grand."

"Excuse me?"

"Okay, I'll knock about two hundred off the bill since the kid is sort of cute."

"Please tell me you're joking."

"I also take major credit cards."

She stared at him.

"I'm joking." He tweaked her cheeks and then realized what he'd done. "Sorry. I'd gotten in the habit of doing that this evening."

Leila exhaled and then laughed at their exchange. "Not a problem. You had me going there for a minute."

Garrick turned and headed back down the hall and descended the staircase. "So how did it go?" he asked.

She followed close behind him. "I'm sorry?"

He stopped at the base. "Dinner. How was the meeting?"

She sighed. "It didn't quite go as I expected."

"Sorry to hear it." He stood there not sure why he wasn't heading for the door. Then again, maybe it had something to do with her magnificent dress or the sweet scent that clung to her hair and skin.

"Well, I'll survive." She laughed and rolled her eyes. "That sounded corny, didn't it?"

He hesitated.

"Great." She turned from him and went toward the kitchen. "I need something to drink. Maybe a glass of wine will do it. Care to join me?"

Garrick glanced at his watch again and shrugged. "Sure. What the heck?"

Chapter 8

"They want me to sell my magazine," Leila confessed and sat before the fireplace.

Garrick settled down in front of her, popped the cork to a bottle of pinot grigio, and then poured two glasses. "So what are you going to do?"

She opened her mouth to declare she was going to tell Hearst they could cram their offer, but instead she said, "I don't know."

He handed her a glass.

"It's a very good offer," she admitted. "A part of me thinks it's crazy to walk away. The other part…I don't know." She glanced up and was warmed by the intensity of his gaze. "You know, I'm constantly going on about me or my family problems. I hardly know anything about you."

He frowned.

"I mean other than the stuff on your credit or police report. By the way, you might want to hurry and pay that speeding ticket you received six months ago."

Garrick rocked his head back with a hearty laugh. "Thanks for the reminder." He sipped his wine. "So what do you want to know?"

"Tell me about your work." She twirled the contents in her glass. "Pretend I don't know what you do for a living."

"All right." He eased down onto his side and gazed up at her. "I'm an architect and just took over as president of my father's firm about six months ago. I love designing buildings, however, I'm not too fond of the managing aspect."

"Really? I love it."

"I bet you do." He chuckled. "You probably run your magazine with an iron fist."

"No…I can be flexible," she defended slyly. "I'm fair, levelheaded—most of the time."

"And if I was to ask your employees?"

She hesitated. "They may have a *slightly* different view of things."

They laughed.

Stunned, Garrick recognized the same musical notes Emma emitted during one of her belly laughs. When he turned up his glass again, he delighted in the way the light from the crackling fire danced in her eyes and illuminated her honey-coated skin. Her exposed shoulders enticed to the point where his fingers itched to touch them.

"Have you ever been married?" Leila asked out of the blue.

"You mean your little P.I. work didn't turn up that information?"

She bit her lower lip and pretended to play coy. "Maybe."

"I'm divorced." Their eyes met and he could see there was another question she wanted to ask; but she didn't, and he was relieved. "What about you? Have you ever been married?"

"No, but I was engaged once. Came to my senses about a week before the nuptials, gave the ring back, and lived happily ever after."

"No regrets?" he asked.

"Pertaining to marriage—no." She drew a deep breath and drained the rest of her glass. "It's been my experience that men have a real problem with career women."

His eyes drifted to his glass. "Oh?"

She nodded and observed him. "You'd be amazed how many men still want their women to be barefoot, pregnant, and catering to their every whim. I mean, this is the twenty-first century. You would think we wouldn't have to explain the need or the desire to accomplish something more than baking cookies."

"What about the desire to plant roots—watch something grow?"

"I still have that option, but I resent the assumption I can't do both."

"Equally?" He laughed, and then caught himself.

"Men do both," she challenged.

He sat up. "It's not the same. When a child comes into the world, women are programmed to be the nurturers—"

"You've been spouting that nonsense so long you actually believe it."

"Men can have babies now?"

"That's not what I'm saying." She set her glass down and massaged her neck to camouflage her irritation.

"You're upset."

"No. No," she lied.

Garrick gave in to the temptation and reached for her hand; however, she skillfully dodged his touch. "Okay." He also set down his glass. "I'll take that as my cue to exit stage left."

"Women are blessed with the ability to procreate," she continued.

He held his tongue, realizing he stood on thin ice.

"But don't shoot off some sexist male agenda about how we're the only ones programmed to stay up all night, prep bottles, and change dirty diapers."

"You're right," Garrick acquiesced. "*You* were never programmed to do those things."

"You were. Imagine that." She smiled despite herself. "But I'm serious."

"I can see that." He paused and then reached for his glass again.

"So you disagree with me?" She folded her arms and kept her gaze leveled on him.

"I didn't say that."

"You didn't have to." Leila shook her head. "So what happened?"

"What—to my marriage?"

She nodded. "You look more like the 'till death do we part' type, so I'm guessing—?"

"You don't beat around the bush, do you?" Garrick chuckled to hide his discomfort.

Her cheeks darkened at the polite reprimand. "Sorry. You don't have to answer that."

He reached for the bottle of wine while he thought the question over. "Truth is, even though I lived through it, I don't know what happened." He refilled his glass and then reached for hers. "I remember the arguments, but never the cause. I remember us lying in bed, but feeling lonely. Then I remember her asking for a divorce and being incredibly relieved."

"I'm sorry," she whispered.

"Don't be." He sucked in a long breath. "I'm not."

Leila studied him and then set her drink aside. "I better not. Emma may wake up tonight." She removed the pins from her head. "Though I hope not."

Garrick watched, fascinated, as her thick mane tumbled around her shoulders. Again, his fingers itched; this time to run through her hair.

Even though the last thing Leila needed was some desperate-housewives scenario where she was sleeping with her next-door neighbor, she couldn't stop herself from flirting.

This evening, she ran a gamut of emotions and the ones that streamed through her now reminded her that she was just a girl, sitting before a boy, wishing he would strip off her clothes. Gee, how long had it been since she'd been in a relationship?

For a long while, the soft crackle from the fireplace remained as the only sound in the room. She lowered her gaze and pretended that her thoughts had drifted. In truth, she mentally measured the length of his hands and tried to guesstimate his shoe size.

"Hey?"

Leila surfaced from the sea of forbidden thoughts and prayed he wouldn't read her mind again.

"Where did you go this time?" he asked.

She blushed before thinking of a lie and he saw straight through her.

"It's late. I better go." He climbed to his feet, and then offered a hand to help her up.

"Oh, okay." She blinked in surprise. *What happened?*

He pulled her up with too much strength and she smacked into his chest. The wonderful smell of soap and aftershave lingered on his skin. The very essence of him invaded her senses and she quaked from the knees up.

Seducing her neighbor was not smart, but damn if she could think of anything other than slipping out of her dress.

"You're a very beautiful woman," he admitted in a husky whisper. "Something tells me you know that."

Her eyes skirted up his broad chest, thick neck, cleft chin, and then finally met his warm gaze. "You're a good-looking man—and I'm sure you know that as well."

His eyes lowered to her lips and she practiced restraint by not running her tongue across them.

"The holidays are rough for people who aren't in relationships," he reasoned.

"Are you suggesting I'm only attracted to you because I'm lonely?"

"No. I'm asking."

She crooked up one corner of her mouth and leaned into him. "Does it matter?"

Garrick remained hypnotized by her lips and she could literally feel his indecision pulse through the air between them.

"What about you?" she asked, hoping to influence his verdict. "Are you lonely?"

The fire's crackle grew louder as she watched the slow descent of his head. Her stomach twisted with anticipation while her knees threatened to give out. She sighed when his lips finally caressed her own to intoxicate her more than the wine.

Leila slid her hands up his chest and then looped them around his neck. She dangled from a magical cloud and he was an old wish materialized.

The hunger in his kiss demanded something she wasn't sure she wanted to give. His strong hands emoted more than strength—more than security. Suddenly, she realized she was in over her head.

Her imagination took hold of her and snapshots of mind-blowing sex filled her head. Her body ached, but she wanted him to make the next move.

Once again, Emma proved she had perfect or rather lousy timing. Leila wasn't sure of which.

Garrick ended the kiss and sounded like a man who'd just completed the Peachtree Road Race.

She, too, couldn't catch her breath and, worse, she was already feeling signs of addiction. "I better go check on Emma," she whispered.

He swallowed and nodded.

"Are you going to be here when I get back?"

Once again, he appeared fascinated by her lips; but after a moment, he shook his head. "I don't think that's a wise idea. What will the neighbors think?"

She tried to smile, but her disappointment prevented her. "Then I'll go ahead and say good-night."

Garrick leaned forward and she closed her eyes, waiting for the last taste of sin. Instead, his lips brushed against her forehead.

Her eyes flew open in shock, yet she held her tongue as he turned away and headed toward the front door. She collected herself and followed.

Emma quieted; undoubtedly she'd fallen back to sleep. However, the damage had already been done and the night's stardust had faded.

At the open door, Garrick turned toward her. "Don't forget, if you need anything—"

"You'll be the first person I'll call."

He nodded, lingered for a moment, and then finally crossed the threshold and stepped into the black velvet night.

"Bye," she said.

"Good night."

She smiled and watched him cross the street before she closed and locked the door. She immediately reminisced on their kiss and a glorious warmth returned. "Until next time."

Chapter 9

Garrick couldn't sleep.

How could he with so many erotic thoughts of his neighbor floating around in his head? *I did the right thing*. However, his body disagreed.

She wanted him, that much he knew for sure. There was no question what he wanted; but in that one moment when he could have taken it, his head had jarred with warning bells.

Leila Owens was a career woman. It didn't take a rocket scientist to know she ate, slept and lived *Atlanta Spice* magazine. For all her talk about women being able to juggle career and family, she showed no signs of ever exercising the second option.

Of course, there was nothing stopping him from having a casual fling—other than a severe case of common sense. Plus, at his age, he needed something more than just the physical. He liked being in a relationship. Being a yang to someone's yin. He needed a deeper connection. Something spiritual as well as physical.

Garrick cleared his thoughts and laughed. Undoubtedly, he would be a hopeless romantic to the end. Against his will, his mind looped an image of Leila peeling out of her white sequined dress and revealing a physique that had *all* his body parts itching to touch her.

He closed his eyes and could still taste her wine-flavored lips and feel her heartbeat against his chest. She had awakened something in him and he was torn on what he wanted to do about it.

Garrick tossed around, pounded his pillow, and still sleep eluded him. It didn't make any sense; he hardly knew the woman…and she was everything he didn't want in a partner.

"Lord, save me from gold diggers and career-driven women," he mumbled. However, he had a sneaky suspicion his prayer fell on deaf ears.

Time crept at a snail's pace until dawn colored the horizon. Only then did Garrick's eyelids grow heavy with sleep; yet, Leila refused to be banished from his thoughts. Her sweet, floral-scented hair and her classic perfume flooded his senses while her wonderful belly laugh played like music in his ears.

On the second day Leila strolled through the doors of *Atlanta Spice* with a baby in her arms, she received just as many stares as she had on the first. Until she hired a nanny, she was stuck between a rock and a hard place.

Like the previous day, Emma charmed members of her staff with her chubby cheeks, wide brown eyes and her infectious laugh.

"I see you survived another night," Ciara said, breezing into Leila's office with a stack of copy-edits. "Or should I say, just barely? You need to put some cucumbers on your eyes for those bags."

"Thanks for the beauty tip."

"Did Emma keep you up? How did your meeting go? Did you get your hunky neighbor to babysit? Have you jumped his bones yet?"

"Whoa. Whoa. One question at a time." Leila placed Emma inside her playpen. "And how are you going to ask about my jumping someone's bones in front of my niece?"

"She doesn't know what we're talking about."

Leila drew a deep, patient breath as she made it around to her desk. "Children are like sponges. They absorb everything," she echoed and then remembered who had told her that.

"Is that right?" Ciara's eyebrows rose in surprise as she folded her arms. "You're a surrogate mom for five days and already you're an expert on child behavior?" Her smile widened. "I have to remember to write this day down for the history books."

"Ha. Ha. Not funny." Leila settled into her chair and booted up her computer. "The answer to your question is no."

"To which question?"

Leila dropped her elbows onto her desk and pinched the bridge of her nose. "Okay, let's start from the beginning. Emma slept through the night. The meeting was a disaster. Yes, I had my hunky next-door neighbor to babysit. And *no,* I didn't jump his bones."

"Oh." Ciara frowned. "What happened at the meeting?"

Leila drew another breath and relayed every painstaking detail of her business dinner with Mr. Porter. When she finished, Ciara looked shell-shocked.

"I'm going to be laid off?" She blinked. "But I'm pregnant. I need the health-care benefits."

"Calm down. No one is being laid off. I'm not going to accept their offer."

"You're going to turn down sixty-five million dollars? Are you crazy?"

"It's not about the money," Leila huffed, and glanced over at Emma, who drooled on her stuffed frog. "Some things are more important than that."

Ciara followed her gaze and then glanced back at her boss. "Are we talking about the same thing here?"

Leila's gaze shifted to Ciara. "*Atlanta Spice* isn't for sale. It's my dream. It's my heart. It's my everything."

"You don't have a plan B, do you?"

A sad smile ghosted around Leila's lips while she shook her head. "I put all my eggs in this one basket."

"Yeah, but it's one hell of a basket."

"What? You're encouraging me to sell now?"

Emma scrunched up her face and started to cry.

Leila's body deflated as she exhaled in exhaustion. "I still hadn't had my morning cup of coffee."

"I'm right on it." Ciara turned and marched toward the door, stopping briefly to pinch Emma's cheek.

Emma's fake cries stopped long enough for her eyes to follow Leila's secretary out the door.

"I knew you were a faker," Leila smirked.

Emma turned back and looked at her aunt through the pen's mesh netting and giggled.

"Okay, we need to come to an understanding, young lady." Leila leaned forward in her desk. "I need for you to be on your best behavior."

Her niece nodded.

"Good. I have to find a new distributor, hire you a nanny, and find your mother. Oh, yeah, and run a magazine."

Emma giggled again.

"I'm serious. You do me this favor…and I'll personally pay for your college education." Leila studied her. "Do we have a deal?"

Emma nodded and gurgled nonsense.

"I'm going to take that as a yes."

Twenty minutes later, all deals were off.

As soon as Leila jumped on the phone, Emma screamed bloody murder. No amount of bouncing or patting soothed her and the child ignored all stuffed animals and toys.

Ciara stepped in, but she, too, was at a loss as to what was wrong with the child.

"Ciara, find me a mother in this office and get her in here quick. I have a conference call in five minutes."

"You got it."

"Oh, baby. Please. What's wrong?"

Emma's screams heightened while fat crocodile tears leaked from her eyes.

Leila retrieved the pink diaper bag and pulled out every toy she could find. Nothing worked. "Baby, please don't do this to me," she moaned. "Can't you just tell me what's wrong?"

Her niece took mercy and downgraded her

outburst to loud, spasmodic sniffles and Leila waylaid hitting the panic button.

A hard knock disrupted the peace and Emma once again filled her lungs and belted another ear-piercing scream.

"Come in," Leila shouted, praying for someone who knew what to do; instead, Mr. Porter glided through the door.

He entered and froze in his tracks. "Is this a bad time?"

She blinked. "Uh, no," Leila said. "C'mon in." Mentally, she finally hit her panic button and rushed over to her desk to buzz for Ciara.

Of course, Ciara wasn't at her desk.

"So." She turned to face Porter. "What brings you by?"

Emma kicked and tried to shimmy out of her aunt's arms.

Porter frowned at the screaming baby and then smacked his hand against his face. "Well, I feel foolish. I went on and on about the ticking of your biological clock and you've already beat the alarm."

"What?"

"Your baby." He chuckled awkwardly.

"No, uh, this is my niece. I'm sort of watching her for a while." She buzzed Ciara again.

"Oh." He winced as the child discovered a new octave, and then glanced around.

"Please have a seat," she offered and resumed bouncing and patting.

Porter hesitated, but then lowered into the leather couch against the wall. Something squeaked and he jumped up. He turned around and plucked Emma's rubber ducky from the chair.

Leila flushed with embarrassment. "Sorry about that."

"Not a problem." Porter waved off her concerns. "Used to happen to me all the time at home."

"Leila, I found..." Ciara tugged Sylvia from the reception desk in behind her. "I'm sorry. I didn't have Mr. Porter on your schedule."

"Just dropped by, actually," he shouted.

Sylvia rushed over to Leila and extracted Emma. "I'll take her so you two can talk."

"I think that I may need to take her to a pediatrician," Leila said.

Sylvia felt Emma's head. "She does have a

slight fever." Next she stuck her finger in the child's mouth, and then smiled. "Ah, I know what's wrong with you."

"You do?" Leila's shoulders slumped with visible relief.

"Sure do." Sylvia nodded with a broad grin. "She's teething."

Chapter 10

"I'm telling you, you're going to love Vanessa," Tamara boasted as she unloaded groceries into Garrick's refrigerator. "I wrote up a list of pros and cons last night and I'm convinced you two will be married within a year."

Garrick's eyebrows jumped to the center of his forehead while he was in mid chug from his Gatorade bottle.

"Now, I know you're thinking I must be crazy, but I've thought long and hard about this," she continued without sparing him a glance. "You were right the other day."

He drained the rest of the bottle and dragged the back of his hand across his mouth. "About what?"

"You needing a stay-at-home wife."

"I never said that. There's a big difference from a woman with a job and a woman obsessed with climbing the corporate ladder."

Tamara rolled her eyes. "Whatever. My point is—you need someone to look after you. I mean, there are more items in a grocery store than hot dogs and Gatorade."

Garrick's back stiffened. "I was going shopping right after my workout." He gestured to his sweat-soaked workout clothes.

"You couldn't prove it by me." Tamara laughed and moved to stock the cabinets. "Anyway, Vanessa has been a widow for five years and I've convinced her it's time for her to get back into the dating scene."

"Is that right?" He settled at the breakfast bar. "You're a regular little busybody, aren't you?"

She shrugged. "There's nothing wrong with looking out for my loved ones, is there?"

Garrick smiled.

"Besides," she continued. "Vanessa is perfect. She's smart, beautiful and, other than her charity work, she wants to be a stay-at-home mom."

"Children?"

Tamara stopped to flash a dimpled smile. "No, but she mentioned to me the other day about hearing her biological clock ticking."

"Well, looks like you have everything covered. Just tell me the wedding date and I'll be there."

"Very funny." She folded her arms. "If you think I'm being pushy, you can tell me."

He hesitated.

"You do, don't you?" Her voice rose defensively. "If you want, I'll call Vanessa right now and cancel—"

Garrick chuckled as he held up his hand. "No. No. It's just that maybe you're moving things a little too fast."

"But—"

"In five minutes you've predicted marriage within a year, how bad the woman's biological clock is ticking, and I haven't even *met* her yet."

Tamara opened her mouth for rebuttal, but when none came, she closed her mouth and slumped in defeat. "You're right."

"I'm what?" He blinked.

"Don't gloat." She shut the cabinet door and crossed the kitchen to join him at the breakfast bar. "I just want you to be happy," she said. "After Miranda—I just feel sort of responsible."

"Responsible?"

"I did introduce you two, remember?"

Touched, Garrick reached for her hand. "I had no idea you felt that way." He studied her and thought for the millionth time that his brother was a lucky man. "Miranda and I weren't right for each other. We married for all the wrong reasons. It's nobody's fault. The most important thing is that she's happy and…"

Tamara caught his hesitation. "Are you happy?"

He thought about giving her a fluff answer, but the moment called for honesty. "I think I'm at a crossroad," he admitted.

"What do you mean?" She leaned forward and sandwiched his hand.

Garrick thought for a moment. "I think

you're right. I do need someone to take care of me, but more importantly I love taking care of a woman. I want to be someone's rock. It's nice feeling needed, you know?"

"What?"

He shook off his musing. "Nothing. Don't worry about me. I'll be fine."

He sighed when Leila's face surfaced in his mind. "The funny thing is—what I thought I didn't want may be the very thing I need."

At wits end, Leila canceled all her appointments and returned home with a full-fledged migraine. At least Emma finally cut her a break and fell asleep during the ride.

"God knew what he was doing when he made babies cute. Otherwise, it just isn't worth the trouble," she said with a smile and unbuckled the car seat. She extracted Emma and closed the car door, but before she headed toward the house, Garrick, with his arm draped around a woman, caught her attention.

The lady looked familiar, but Leila had a hard time placing the face from across the street. Judging by their body language, and she felt like an expert, the two were extremely comfortable with each other.

Pure unadulterated jealousy surprised Leila and curdled her stomach. Just last night, he'd had his arms wrapped around her and his mouth…

Garrick looked up and caught Leila's stare. He smiled and thrust up his chin as if to ask *what's up?*

Embarrassed to have been caught staring, Leila fluttered a smile, and then turned away. Careful and conscious not to race like a scared rabbit back to the house, she took her time to stroll in long, measured steps with her head held high.

Even as she did so, she felt the weight of Garrick's stare follow her. On one hand, she would give anything to know what he was thinking and on the other, she wondered why she should care.

Once she made it inside and closed the door, she exhaled before her lungs exploded. However, her curiosity about Garrick and the mystery lady failed to wane. She set the car seat down next to the door and turned to peer out the peephole.

"Where is he?" She squinted and moved around, trying to locate him. Unsuccessful, she walked over to the glass paneling next to the door. Leila finally spotted Garrick, standing and laughing with his female friend. Her jealousy returned in full force.

Leila's gaze raked the competition and she frowned. *Competition?* Was she seriously interested in her neighbor—especially after his rejection last night? And it was rejection. She couldn't have been more clear about what she wanted if she'd had glowing orange lights directing him to the bedroom.

And he had turned her down.

Last night, Garrick had talked of his divorce, but she'd failed to ask key questions like: Was he dating someone serious? It would make sense. A man like Garrick Grayson wouldn't be on the market long—even if he did need a lesson in women's studies. Leila considered the shapely woman and then sucked in a painful gasp when Garrick leaned forward and kissed the woman.

Leila stepped back, but didn't turn away.

He opened the car door and Leila watched as his friend sank behind the wheel and pulled out of the drive. Once the car disappeared, Garrick looked across the street and, for a brief moment, Leila believed their gazes met.

Slowly, he turned away to stroll back to his door. It was Leila's turn to watch his stride and appreciate his well-defined body.

Emma squirmed in her chair and drew Leila's attention. Luckily, the child remained asleep and when Leila looked out the window, Garrick was gone.

"I need to get a grip," she mumbled, and then walked away from the window.

Roslyn loved Barbados. For the past week, she and her family had entertained fantasies of living the rest of their lives on the tranquil island. It felt good to be separated from the regular hustle and bustle of the holidays and to just enjoy the basics: her family.

She lounged on the beach's white sand and was lulled between sleep and consciousness when her six-year-old daughter, Courtney, raced up to her from the water.

"Mommy, we forgot to call Aunt Leila again to wish her a Merry Christmas."

Roslyn moaned lazily, not wanting to open her eyes. "It's okay, honey. Remember, your aunt Leila doesn't like to celebrate Christmas."

"Well that's just silly." Courtney frowned. "Everyone celebrates Christmas."

Roslyn didn't have the heart to correct her daughter on that belief. "Trust me. Aunt Leila is probably buried with work at her office. She likes it like that."

Courtney screwed up her face. "She works too much."

Roslyn opened her eyes and slid off her shades. "I agree." She looked out into the water and spotted her husband splashing around with their four-year-old daughter, Breanna, and smiled.

"What about Aunt Samantha? Are we going to call her?"

I would if I could. "Tell you what—" she sat up and took Courtney's hand "—I can't promise you we can reach Aunt Samantha, but let's go and call your aunt Leila at work. Will that make you feel better?"

Courtney nodded.

Roslyn couldn't resist pinching her daughter's cheeks. "Okay. Let's go give her a call."

* * *

Leila was not enjoying the whole teething experience—and whoever invented those damn biscuits-slash-cookies that dissolved into a gooey mess needed to be shot. However, Leila's saving grace was having an endless supply of baby wipes.

One thing for sure, she wasn't going to get any work done at home, either. Emma made it clear that while her pediatric Anbesol was working, she wanted to be entertained. Leila exchanged her work clothes for loose-fitting sweat clothes and, in no time, nearly every inch of the living-room floor was covered with toys.

As it turned out, Emma enjoyed sticking everything she could get her hands on into her mouth. She also giggled up a storm whenever Leila blew raspberries against her belly.

The afternoon flew by and Leila forgot about work, finding a nanny, Samantha, and even Garrick. *What would it be like to have a little mini me running around the house?* The renegade thought carved a smile across her lips.

The telephone rang.

"Oh, who can that be?" she asked Emma, and then scooped her off the floor. "Hello."

"Hello, Leila?"

"Sam?" Leila snapped out of her baby fog. "I'm going to kill you. Where the hell are you?"

"No. It's me, Roslyn," her sister corrected. "I was calling because Courtney wanted to talk with you. Wait a minute." Roslyn's voice morphed with concern. "Have you heard from Sam or something?"

Leila laughed. "Oh, I've heard from her all right." She quickly told her sister about her surprise Christmas gift and the subsequent sleepless nights thereafter.

Roslyn fell silent.

"Hello. Are you still there?"

"Please tell me you're joking," her sister finally said.

Emma grabbed the phone cord and garbled out some nonsense.

"Then it's true," Roslyn said. "Ms. Friedman said she saw Sam with a baby, but Patrick—"

"You mean to tell me that you knew?" Leila snapped.

"I suspected, but I didn't have any concrete evidence. I even tried to tell you—but I certainly didn't think she'd do something like abandon the child with you. Even you have to admit that's a bit far-fetched, even for Sam."

Leila huffed and rolled her eyes.

"But how are you holding up?"

"How do you think? I don't know anything about babies. Why didn't she dump her at your place?"

"Maybe because I'm out of town," Roslyn reasoned. "Has she been giving you much trouble?"

Leila glanced down at her wide-eyed niece and felt a tug of guilt about tattling about their transition period. "No. She hasn't been any trouble."

Emma flashed a wide, dimpled smile, and then tried to put the phone cord into her mouth.

"But you're still going to be back on January second, right?"

Roslyn laughed. "I take it that you want me to take over?"

To avoid a guilt trip, this time, Leila didn't look at her niece. "Let's face it. You're the more reasonable choice. You have kids. Meanwhile, I can concentrate on finding Samantha."

"Sam is a master at the disappearing act.

You're not going to be able to find her unless she wants to be found."

It was the truth and Leila knew it.

"But I'll still take little Emma off your hands if you want."

Guilt needled its way into Leila's head. "Well, it's just that I have a company to run and all."

"There's no need to explain," Roslyn assured. "I completely understand."

The guilt now spread through her body like a cancer; but it wasn't as if she were lying—she did have a company to run.

"Well, I can't wait to meet Emma," Roslyn continued. "It will even be good to have a baby in the house again."

Leila concluded she wasn't feeling well. Suddenly, she was jealous at the thought that Emma would prefer to live with Roslyn rather than herself. That was silly, right?

Chapter 11

A nervous Garrick arrived for his blind date with Vanessa Hunter dressed to impress and with the customary bundle of flowers. As he approached the door, he still wasn't certain this was something he was ready to do. Then again, was there really a right time to jump into the shark-infested waters of dating?

He drew a deep breath, said a quick prayer, and rang the doorbell. The moment he did so, he wished he hadn't. Anxiety twisted his stomach into knots and his prepared speech jumbled in his head. Before he could do anything about it, the door opened and Garrick's eyes traveled skyward.

"Hello. Vanessa?"

The extremely tall woman nodded, leaving him to wonder what the hell his sister-in-law was thinking. His gaze took in the woman's broad face, wide nose and pencil-thin mustache and his mind drew a blank. While it was true that beauty was in the eye of the beholder, Garrick couldn't behold anything past what looked like a large Adam's apple. Surely, he was mistaken.

"Would you like to come in?" she asked in a low, husky baritone.

He stood there unable to answer the question.

"Oh, are those for me?" she asked, glancing down at the flowers.

Garrick snapped out of his reverie and broadcast a wide facial smile as he offered her the flowers. "I hope, er, you like them."

"They're beautiful." Vanessa inhaled their fresh fragrance, and then glanced over their short petals to smile at him. "Tamara told me you were a gentleman."

"It seems she forgot to tell me..." Garrick

blinked and shifted gears when Vanessa's eyebrows rose inquisitively. "She forgot to tell me how tall you are."

Vanessa smiled. "I bet you don't date too many women who are my height."

"I can honestly say you'll be the first." His smile tightened as he continued to stare at the troublesome bulge in the center of her throat.

"I better go put these in some water," she hinted. "Do you think you're ready to come in now?"

He hesitated again, but then convinced himself he was overreacting. "Certainly. I would love to come in."

One of Leila's favorite and recent purchases was a handcrafted deluxe glider rocking chair. She couldn't remember anything that felt as good as having her niece nestled on her chest while she hummed along with a Fisher-Price lullaby monitor.

I could get used to this.

She stopped rocking and questioned her sanity. For the past six days, Leila's life had been hijacked, her nerves frayed, and her addiction to coffee had increased tenfold. Yet, there were snatches of time, like now, when she felt this…longing.

That didn't make any sense either. She chuckled under her breath and resumed rocking. Leila, a go-getter from birth, had accomplished everything she had ever set out to do. She was a success—despite her early circumstances.

The last thing she needed—or even wanted— was a child. The backs of her eyes stung unexpectedly, as if she was calling herself a liar. She blinked back the tears, while her thoughts shifted gears. "I would make a lousy mom," she reasoned.

"I mean, look at me." She shrugged. "At best I'm emotionally high-strung and at worst I'm an emotional wreck. That's not a good quality to look for in a mother. Trust me." Nicole Owens's face surfaced in Leila's mind. "I know."

Leila reached over and shut off the music. The ensuing silence felt like a balm to her restless soul; but out of the stillness, she experienced a moment of clarity. Samantha had to have felt the same way.

Leila closed her eyes, drew a deep breath

and, when she exhaled, a few tears finally trickled from her eyes. Eight-year-old Samantha had had the unfortunate honor of discovering their mother's lifeless body; ten-year-old Roslyn had found the pills; and twelve-year-old Leila had found the suicide letter.

She glanced down at Emma. The thought of motherhood must have terrified Sam, just as it did Leila. The one trait they had inherited from their mother.

Pushing her troubled thoughts to the back of her head, Leila stood and carefully placed her niece into bed. After she checked the baby monitor, she stepped out of the room and closed the door.

In the kitchen, she cleaned and sanitized baby bottles until her hands turned into wrinkled prunes. While doing the laundry, she was amazed about the amount of clothes, bibs, burp cloths and blankets that had piled up in just six days.

After tackling that task, Leila took a hot shower, slid into her favorite pajamas, twisted a towel like a turban on her head, and then applied her weekly mud mask. Since she wasn't going to be able to go to work, she would have to do her work at home.

"Now what did I do with my briefcase?" She searched around the living room before remembering that she'd brought the diaper bag in but not the briefcase. "I'm never going to be able to remember all of this."

She donned her robe and her favorite fuzzy slippers and rushed out to the car to retrieve her briefcase. When she reached the car, she heard a door slam across the street.

As luck would have it, Leila and Garrick looked up at the same time.

She smiled.

He frowned.

"The mask." Her hand flew to her face and horror rushed through her body. She pivoted and sprinted back to her door—only to find it locked. "No. Damn it, no."

She banged on the door and even thought about kicking it; but it wasn't as if Emma were going to crawl out of her crib to come answer the door.

"Is there a problem?" Garrick asked.

Leila's eyes widened to the size of silver dollars. "No. Everything is fine," she squeaked, refusing to turn around.

A long silence drifted between them for a

moment before he finally asked, "So why won't you go into the house?" He was behind her.

She continued to stare wide-eyed at the door while her brain scrambled for something—anything—to say. "I, uh, seem to have locked myself out."

A deep rumble of laughter completed her shame. "It's not funny."

"Sorry." He cleared his throat. "But after a night like I had, I find everything funny."

Leila said nothing.

"I take it you don't have a spare key stashed around here somewhere?"

"That would be too easy, don't you think?"

He laughed again.

"Please, don't," she begged, leaning her forehead against the door.

"Okay, we can think through this," he said. "Of course I'd rather not brainstorm with your back."

Leila allowed another wave of silence to crash between them.

"Won't you turn around?"

"I'd rather not."

Garrick expelled a long, frustrated sigh. "And why not?"

"Because I'm hideous."

He frowned. "Excuse me?"

Her shoulders slumped with defeat while she squeezed her eyes shut. "Promise me you won't laugh," she groaned.

"Okay."

"No. You have to say it."

"All right." He paused. "I promise."

Resolved and determined to get the humiliation over with, Leila turned around and waited. When he said nothing, she finally peeled her eyes open only to find him smiling at her.

"You said you wouldn't laugh."

He held on to his smile. "I'm not laughing," he said defensively.

"You want to laugh."

"True," he admitted. "But since I gave you my word, I'm not going to."

She tilted her chin up in a desperate attempt to hold on to her pride. "I appreciate that."

"Of course, I also want to point out that I also didn't laugh the first day we met when you wore the same outfit and you had your hair sticking straight up."

Leila's hand shot up to her head, but she was

relieved to feel the towel still wrapped around her head. "Then I want to go on record that I think it's in bad taste to bring that up now."

"Sorry." His smile turned into a smirk. "Although I think it's very important that people learn not to take themselves too serious. You have to learn to laugh at yourself."

"Really?" She crossed her arms. "I bet that's easy for you to say, since you have so much dirt on me. I have nothing on you."

"Okay." He hesitated and then drew a deep breath. "How about this—my sister-in-law set me up on a blind date tonight with a transvestite."

Leila's bark of laughter was out of her mouth before she could think.

"See?" He straightened and squared his shoulders. "Very funny, isn't it? I hope she thinks so, too, when I strangle her."

"That woman I saw you with earlier—?"

"My sister-in-law, Tamara."

Leila rolled her eyes when she realized that she had been jealous of the man's sister-in-law.

"What is it?" he asked.

"Nothing." She chuckled. "It's just me being silly."

Garrick rolled up his sleeves. "Well, let's see if we can get you into the house so we can check on little Emma, shall we?"

"That would be nice."

After checking all the windows, Garrick raced to his place and returned with a small nail kit. In less than two minutes, he'd unlocked her door.

"How did you do that?"

"Let's just say my brother and I fell into a little trouble from time to time when we were younger."

She frowned.

"Don't worry. I grew out of it." He winked and then inched closer. "So how about a night-cap?"

Leila thought about the previous night's rejection and even about his *bad* date. What was she supposed to be—some type of consolation prize?

"Actually, I have a lot of work I need to catch up on. Speaking of which, I almost forgot again." She rushed back out to the car and retrieved her briefcase.

A smiling Garrick remained rooted by the door when she returned.

"Rain check?" he asked.

"Sure." She shrugged.

Garrick waited until her skittering gaze met his again. In an instant, she nearly drowned in the dark pools of his eyes and her breath thinned to a dangerous level. When he leaned forward, she guessed what was about to happen next and she had a half a heartbeat to decide whether to stop him.

She didn't.

Leila sighed when the soft petals of his lips landed against hers. Her knees jittered and she slid a hand up against his chest for support. To her surprise, she felt the wild pounding of his heart.

When the kiss ended, she took a step back to clear her head, but it didn't work.

"I hope you didn't mind," he said, retreating and expanding the distance between them.

"Uh, no. I rather enjoyed it." She tried to smile, but her mud mask had hardened like cement. Leila cupped a hand to her face. "I better go and wash this stuff off. Good night." She turned.

Garrick gently restrained her by the hand.

She looked back.

"I enjoyed it, too," he said, and then released her. "Good night." He turned and walked away.

Chapter 12

"How could you forget about Opulence's New Year charity party?" Ciara questioned over the phone.

"How do you think?" Leila rolled her eyes as her airplane maneuver with oatmeal missed its destination and crashed against the side of Emma's face.

The child promptly reached out and dug her fingers into the food.

"No, no, Emma." Leila tried to pry her niece's fingers from the baby spoon, but Emma proved victorious and snatched it and waved it around.

Oatmeal flew everywhere—again.

"Give me that." Leila grabbed for the spoon and didn't see Emma reach for the bowl.

"So are you still going?" Ciara asked.

"Of course I'm going. I'm presenting a check to the American Cancer Association on behalf of the magazine. I have to be there."

Emma jerked up the bowl.

Leila gasped when the rest of her niece's breakfast splattered across her face. "Oh, you little hellion."

Emma giggled and then attempted to set the bowl on top of her head.

"Give me that."

"Leila? What happened?" Ciara's concern filtered through the phone.

"Nothing. My darling niece is just showing me her love for abstract art." Leila pulled globs of oatmeal from her hair.

"You're wearing her food, aren't you?"

"Every bit of it." She laughed. "I have to go. It's time to open another box of baby wipes."

"But what are you going to do about a baby-sitter?"

Leila stopped cleaning. "Do I hear an offer?"

"Oh, Leila, I would love to…if Elmo and I didn't already have plans."

She rolled her eyes. "Of course you would."

"But I think I do have a solution for you," Ciara added cheerfully.

"Oh?" Hope pricked Leila's heart.

"My niece, Alison, mentioned to me last night that she was looking to make some extra money. I can ask if she wants to babysit."

"Really?" Leila looked down at Emma, who now tried to shove the plops of oatmeal from the high-chair tray into her mouth. "Does she have any experience?"

"Being the oldest child, she's had to babysit her four brothers from time to time. Since she turned sixteen, I know she's been hired in her neighborhood for babysitting jobs."

"Sixteen?" Leila was more than twice the teenager's age and she could hardly keep up. "I don't know."

"Trust me, Leila," Ciara coaxed. "She's a

very mature sixteen—and who else are you going to find on such short notice?"

Garrick popped to mind, but she quickly dispelled the notion. She'd already made a nuisance of herself.

"Leila?"

"All right. Ask Alison if she can be here by seven-thirty."

"You got it."

"Vanessa is *not* a transvestite!" Tamara thundered, horror-struck.

"I thought she/he looked a little masculine." Orlando grabbed two beers out of the refrigerator and tossed one across the kitchen to his brother.

"And you didn't warn me?" Garrick waited until Orlando was close enough and then popped him on the back of the head.

"Ouch. Tamara said the girl was having some kind of hormone issue," he said, defensively rubbing his head.

"More like testosterone issues."

"Hey!" Tamara popped both of them on the back of the head. "You're talking about my friend."

Garrick moved out of the line of fire. "Tamara, the girl has an Adam's apple larger than mine and Orlando's put together. She's a he."

She jabbed her hands to her hips.

"A very nice he, but a he nonetheless," he added.

"Garrick—!"

"Tamara, how can you be so sure? Have you seen the girl naked?" he asked.

"Have you?" Orlando butted in.

"No." Garrick moved back toward his brother and took another swing.

"Ow. You two are going to give me a concussion."

"Fine." Tamara tossed up her hands. "You're on your own. Find your own dates."

"Now there's a novel idea."

The men tapped their longneck bottles together in a private toast.

"Fine. I can tell when I'm not needed." Tamara shrugged with her bottom lip out. "Why should I care if you die a lonely old man?"

"Uh-oh," Orlando mumbled under his breath. "She's not through."

Garrick sighed. "I'm not going to die a lonely old man."

"Not if I have anything to do with it." She leaned forward and pinched his cheek. "Keira is going to the Baldwins' New Year's Eve party tonight."

"Who?" Orlando and Garrick asked in unison.

"She's another friend of mine. Well, more like an associate. Omara and her daughter attend the same preschool."

Garrick didn't like the direction of this conversation. "And how did I become the subject of conversation at a preschool?"

Tamara's smile widened. "It was all pretty innocent. She was telling me about her rat of an ex-husband and how the only good thing she got out of her marriage was her daughter. Then the conversation went from how even though her first marriage didn't work out, she would love to marry again and have more children. Quite naturally I thought about you and how much you wanted to start a family."

"Quite naturally."

"So you'll do it?"

"No."

Tamara's face scrunched in confusion. "What do you mean? You said things didn't work out with you and Vanessa—so that means you're still on the market. You can't give up just because you had *one* bad date."

"It didn't work out because I don't date men."

"She's not a man!" Tamara glanced guiltily around. "At least I don't think she is."

Garrick shook his head. "My answer is still no."

"What's the big deal? Keira is going to the party and you're going to be at the party. You two can just—"

"I'm not going."

"What? Of course you are."

"I went to one party this season. I met my quota." When his sister-in-law opened her mouth, he continued, "I have a million things to do with work and at the house."

"But—"

"Please." He met her gaze. "Let me do things at my own pace—in my own time."

Tamara stared at him, and then slowly nodded. "Okay."

"Thank you."

Omara stomped her way into the kitchen. "Mommy, you said you were going to come play tea party with me."

An instant smile sprang to Tamara's lips as she grabbed the plastic tea tray from the kitchen counter. "Sorry, sweetheart. Here I come."

Orlando watched his wife and his daughter stroll out of the room before he turned back toward his brother. "Sorry about Vanessa."

"Forget about it." Garrick shrugged and took a swig of his beer.

"And you know Tamara doesn't mean any harm—"

"Yeah, I know."

Orlando bobbed his head. "So what's the real reason you're not going to the party?"

"Work."

"Liar."

Garrick struggled not to smile.

"Maybe I should be asking *who's* the real reason you're not coming to the party tonight?"

"I don't know what you're talking about." Garrick turned up his bottle.

Orlando stared. "Yeah. I just bet you don't."

* * *

Leila had second thoughts the moment Alison showed up at her door. Ciara's very *mature* sixteen-year-old niece had six piercings in each ear and one in her nose. The teenager wore a low-riding hippie skirt and matching tank top. The outfit didn't inspire trust.

"Hello, Ms. Owens." The girl jutted a hand in greeting. "I'm Alison. I'm going to be your babysitter for this evening."

Leila blinked, startled that the young girl had an even younger voice—one more appropriate for a seven-year-old. "I think there's been a mistake."

The girl's shoulders deflated. "I know I'm young, but I assure you that your daughter will be in safe, capable hands."

Leila hedged as she looked down into Alison's eager eyes, and then quickly realized she was overreacting. "Please. Come in." She stepped back and allowed the teenager to enter. "How did you get here?" She glanced out into the driveway.

"A friend dropped me off. Ms. Owens. You look beautiful," Alison exclaimed, changing the subject.

Leila fluttered a hand against her vibrant red dress. "Oh, this old thing?" She winked and closed the door. She quickly ran over her dos and don'ts and disclosed all emergency numbers.

When the limousine arrived, Leila experienced a final flutter of anxiety but then banished it with the affirmation that Ciara wouldn't have sent her niece if she didn't trust the girl herself.

"Good night, Ms. Owens. Enjoy the party." Alison waved from the door.

Leila took a deep breath and fought the urge to run back into the house and perform another double check on the child. She pulled her fur coat close to her body and approached the chauffeur and the limo's open door.

"Good evening, Ms. Owens."

"Good evening." She smiled and then glanced up across the street. When she recognized the figure illuminated in the second-floor window, she waved with a smile and then eased into the car.

Chapter 13

Rooted in front of his bedroom window, Garrick watched in disappointment as the black limousine pulled away from Leila's driveway. In hindsight, it was presumptuous to assume his neighbor didn't have plans for the evening.

He turned and glanced at the tuxedo he'd laid across the bed. "Looks like I won't be needing you." He sighed and left the bedroom to return downstairs.

The heavenly scent of fresh mint and honey wafted throughout the house and churned Garrick's stomach. Once in the kitchen, he opened the oven and removed his signature dish of mint-rubbed leg of lamb and steamed vegetables.

"So much for wowing her with my great culinary skills," he droned. He removed the bottle of champagne he'd set on ice and placed it in the fridge.

A magnet from the local pizza joint caught his attention and he gave serious thoughts to calling them up, but then decided not to waste a perfectly good meal. As he fixed his plate, he couldn't help but remember the number of times he'd cooked or planned an evening with Miranda only to be told at the last minute that she couldn't make it or she'd forgotten about it.

No doubt a magazine founder would have the same hectic schedule. Why was he always attracted to the wrong women?

Garrick shook his head, grabbed a beer, and took his meal up to his home office. In truth, he did have a lot of work to do; but as the minutes ticked on, he discovered that his heart wasn't into it.

After two hours, he pushed back from his

draft table and glanced at his watch. It was nearly ten o'clock. Maybe if he hurried, he could make it to the Baldwins' party before eleven.

There was no sense in bringing in the New Year alone. Of course, there was the horrible thought of meeting that Keira character. He returned the dishes to the kitchen while he weighed his options; even then his thoughts centered on Leila.

Undoubtedly, in the red number peeking out from beneath her coat, the men would be flocking all over her—wherever it was she'd gone for the evening. If she was out having a good time, why shouldn't he?

He bobbed his head in agreement to his own argument and went upstairs to change into his tux. As calculated, he rushed out of the front door at a quarter to eleven; but he'd only made it as far as his car door, when a loud blast of music from across the street caught his ear.

Is that coming from Leila's place?

He glanced around and noticed a crowd of cars at a few of his neighbors'—maybe the music was coming from there. He frowned when he noticed something else: a black Mustang.

That wasn't there earlier, was it?

Garrick stared at the car—wondering.

Finally, he shrugged it off and slid into his car. When he placed his key into the ignition, he stopped. "It wouldn't hurt to just go check things out."

Stepping out of the car, he told himself he was overreacting; yet, it didn't stop him from strolling across the street. The blaring music was coming from Leila's and it didn't sit right. Wasn't Emma there, and shouldn't she be asleep by now?

He rang the doorbell and waited. After a few minutes, Garrick tried the door, relieved and troubled to find it unlocked.

"Hello," he called, entering the house. The music seemed ten times louder inside and he followed its sound. "Hello." He rounded into the living room.

A girl jerked her head up from the couch and screamed.

He jumped as the girl scrambled for her shirt. Before he could say anything, a teenage boy also sat up with a deer-in-headlights expression on his face. Suddenly, everything made sense.

"Who are you? What are you doing here?" the teenage girl asked.

Garrick clenched his jaw as he headed over to the stereo and turned it off. When he did so, Emma's cries and a ringing phone filled the house.

"I'm Garrick Grayson, Ms. Owens's neighbor. And I think it's time you two went home."

Leila flipped her cell phone closed and tried to control her anxiety. Something had to be wrong. Why else would Alison not answer the phone? "I knew this was a bad idea," she mumbled under her breath and exited the ladies' room.

Returning to the main ballroom, she pasted on a broad smile while she navigated around the room to search for her host, Christian Williams.

"Are you sure you have to leave?" Christian, a beautiful woman and cancer survivor, graciously drew Leila aside. "We were going to do the presentations next."

"I know and I'm sorry. But I've been trying to call the babysitter—"

"Oh, Leila." Christian bounced excitedly. "I didn't know you had a baby! Congratulations. Why didn't you tell me?"

"What—?"

Christian turned and called her husband, Jordan, the president of Opulence jewelry, to her side. "Leila had a baby," she announced, clutching her husband.

"No, no." Leila laughed at the misunderstanding and at the idea. "I didn't have a baby."

"But you said—"

"My sister, Samantha, had a baby. I'm just taking care of her daughter—my niece—for a little while."

Christian laughed as her face colored with embarrassment. "I'm sorry." She glanced up at her husband and apologized again. "I misunderstood."

"It's okay. The misunderstanding has been happening a lot."

"Well at least that makes more sense. I can hardly imagine *you* having a baby." Christian laughed.

Leila maintained her smile despite how the comment felt like a kick to the gut. "What do you mean?" she asked.

Christian blinked. "It's just that you've always claimed that motherhood was not for you—remember?" A few inches shaved off Christian's smile as she suddenly looked uncertain. "I didn't mean to imply that you wouldn't make a good mother."

"No, that's not what she meant." Jordan jumped in to defend his wife.

"You're right," Leila proclaimed, letting her friend off the hook. "Motherhood is definitely... not for me." Judging by their faces, she didn't convince them.

Christian cleared her throat and looked nervously at Jordan. A moment of awkward silence hung between the threesome.

"Anyway, I better get going," Leila said.

"No. There's just an hour left to the new year," Jordan protested. "Don't you want to bring it in with us?"

"I would love to—but I need to get home and check on Emma."

"Ten minutes," Christian coerced. "We'll go ahead and do the presentation to the American Cancer Association and then you can go. Deal?"

Leila's bubble of anxiety swelled, but Christian's pleading look worked wonders on her guilt. "Ten minutes," Leila agreed. "Then I'm going home to bring the new year in with my niece."

"Mr. Grayson, are you sure you have to tell Ms. Owens about this? If you do, she'll tell my aunt, and then she will tell my mom—"

Garrick held Emma in his arms as he walked the teenagers to the door. "I'm not unsympathetic to your problem, Alison. But this is about bad decisions, consequences, and taking responsibility for your actions."

Alison's bottom lip sagged. "You're going to tell her."

"I'm going to tell her." He nodded.

"Come on, George. We better go. It's probably going to be the last time you see me until my thirty-fifth birthday."

Garrick smirked as he closed the door behind the teenagers. "Looks like it's you and me, kid."

Emma smiled and made a grab for his tie.

At the sudden constriction of his air supply, Garrick quickly pried her finger loose. "That's a mighty powerful grip you have there, Miss Owens. I'm assuming it's *Owens*."

She clapped her hands and attempted to speak—or sing—or something.

Garrick laughed. "Come on, let's see if we can at least catch the countdown."

It was close to midnight when Leila's limousine pulled up to her house. At least Alison hadn't burned down the house. Now that Leila was back home, it felt ridiculous to have spent all night worrying.

She tipped and thanked the chauffeur for his services and then braced herself before she entered the house. Another wave of relief washed through her at the house's silence.

"Hello…Alison?" Leila strolled through the house still pleased to find nothing was out of place. "Looks like she is responsible," she surmised at seeing the kitchen clean. She glanced again at her watch. The young girl was probably asleep. When she rounded the kitchen's corner, she heard the television in the living room.

The lights were out, a low fire burned in the fire-

place, and the ball was dropping on the flat screen;
but she still didn't see Alison. She approached the
back of the sofa and gasped in surprise.

"Garrick?"

At the sound of his name, Garrick opened his
eyes and smiled lazily up at her. "Good evening,
beautiful."

Leila made another glance around the room.
"What are you doing here?"

"Babysitting," he said simply.

When it was clear that he wasn't going to say
more, she tried again. "*Why* are you babysitting? Where is Alison?"

"I sent her and her *boyfriend* home." He held
on to Emma while he sat up.

"Boyfriend?"

He climbed to his feet. "I'm afraid so. Seems
I walked in on them…playing doctor."

A vibrant color of red flashed before Leila's
eyes. "I'm going to kill her," she growled.

"That's probably not going to be necessary.
She seems to be under the impression that when
you talk to her aunt that she's going to be
grounded for the next couple of decades."

"Are you kidding? I want the girl in pain."

Leila slapped her purse down on the end table and snatched the cordless phone.

"I'll just go put Emma to bed," he whispered while she punched in a phone number.

She stopped in mid-dial. "How is she?"

"What—are you kidding? She's with me." He winked and smiled.

Her anger cooled a few degrees. "Thanks, Garrick. I really appreciate you coming to the rescue. You've been doing that a lot. I don't know how or if I will ever be able to repay you."

He hesitated and then glanced down at Emma. "I'll be right back." He nodded to the phone. "You better make your call."

Something warm and wonderful fluttered in her belly and Leila turned her back to resume dialing. Ciara and her husband didn't answer, but Leila left a brief message about what had happened and urged Ciara to call her first thing in the morning.

When she hung up, Garrick's presence filled the room.

"I put our little girl to bed. How did it go?" he asked.

The wild fluttering returned. "They weren't

home. I left a message." Leila didn't hear him coming up behind her, but she knew if she turned she would be in his embrace.

On the television screen above the fireplace, the countdown for the new year had begun.

"Nine, eight, seven…," the announcer's voice cried out from the television.

She said nothing as Garrick slid her fur coat from her shoulders and tossed it on the sofa. "I love your dress." He glided a finger across her bare shoulder.

Leila shivered at the feel of his breath against the back of her neck.

"I also love it when you pin up your hair."

"Four, three, two…"

Slowly, Leila turned and found her mouth inches from his. She looked into his eyes and could think of nothing but the desire reflected in them as she closed the minuscule distance between them.

"Happy New Year!" The crowd from Times Square cheered.

At that moment, Leila's and Garrick's lips met in a soul-searing kiss.

Chapter 14

Leila moaned as Garrick's mouth roamed over hers with silent authority. She pressed against him and enjoyed the feel of his manhood straining against the lining of his pants. There was something about his guttural groans that heightened her excitement and induced more fog into her brain.

"We shouldn't be doing this," she muttered when she'd mastered enough strength to pull away.

"I know," Garrick agreed. He recaptured her

lips and drove her mouth wide to accept his foraging tongue.

She backed up and bumped into the end table. The lamp toppled over and crashed to the floor.

Leila and Garrick froze. Both waited and strained to hear whether Emma would wake. After a few long heartbeats, the couple looked at each other and laughed.

"Maybe we should slow down?" Leila said, easing away and then around him.

Disappointment etched into Garrick's features, but he managed to nod. "You're right." He licked his lips and ran a hand across the top of his short-cropped hair. "I guess I better get going," he said, yet it sounded more like a question.

"Go?"

He held her gaze. "If that's what you want."

Every system in her body went haywire beneath his dark stare. She, too, licked her lips and loved the way his eyes followed her tongue. "The only place I want you to go is to the other room to the bar. I would like some wine."

A mischievous smile ghosted around his lips as he winked. "I have an idea." He strolled out of the room in long, languid strides.

When he left the room, Leila caught her breath. The man was amazing. If he affected her this way with her clothes on, she couldn't imagine how it would feel with them off. She turned toward the fireplace and turned up the gas. Upstairs, she unearthed a comfortable chenille blanket and returned downstairs to lay it out before the fire. Then it suddenly occurred to her what she was doing.

"Am I going to sleep with him?" she asked herself. She glanced up to see that Garrick had returned in Olympic time. Her eyes roamed over every inch of his fine body and her answer was a resounding: *hell yes*.

"How about champagne?" he asked, holding up a bottle and two glasses.

"Perfect." She walked around to the front of the sofa and found the television remote buried in one of the cushions. She shut off the television and faced him again while he unwrapped the foil on their bottle.

"You look nervous," Garrick said.

"Me? I'm never nervous. Why would I be nervous?"

Leila's pulse jumped when the cork popped

and a stream of champagne ejected from the bottle and spilled out onto the carpet.

"No reason," he said. The same sly grin hugged his lips.

Leila swallowed and crossed the room to stand before him. "You know this is crazy don't you? We hardly know each other."

"I know enough." He filled the two glasses and then handed one to her. "What about you?" He stepped closer.

Suddenly, she didn't trust herself to speak and instead nodded.

"Good. Should we make a toast?"

"What…" She cleared her throat. "What should we toast to? To a happy New Year?"

"Or…we can toast to us." He held up his glass.

Leila hesitated as she nibbled on her bottom lip, and then finally clinked her glass against his. "To us."

Both took a deep gulp of their champagne.

Garrick never took his eyes off her and Leila's body flushed with awareness. This crazy dance they performed drove her crazy, yet at the same time, she anticipated his next move.

"Had enough?"

"I'm sorry?" Her voice cracked.

Garrick only smiled and reached for her glass. "I think you've had enough."

She released her glass and watched as he walked over to the coffee table and set them down.

"Nice blanket." He returned to her side. "Maybe it's time that we made ourselves a little more comfortable." He glided his fingers lazily across her shoulders.

Delicious chills raced through Leila as her eyes grew heavy with passion.

"Look at me," he commanded softly.

She complied, drowning in his eyes.

"I like touching you," he whispered. His fingers shifted direction and now traveled down the center of her chest. "Your skin is so soft," he praised.

Leila inhaled deeply and grew intoxicated by his clean scent. His mere touch crowded all other thoughts from her mind.

"Turn around," he said.

Once again, Leila obeyed and then was surprised by this submissive side of her.

Garrick planted small kisses across her back while he unzipped her dress. "Lovely," he whispered as he peeled the dress off and then let it fall to pool at her feet.

Leila stepped out and kicked the dress aside. She was pleased beyond words that she'd chosen matching satin and lace instead of a mismatched cotton and rayon.

"Do you want to undress me or should I do it?" he asked, drawing the lobe of her ear in between his teeth.

"I'll do it," she panted and turned to face him. She took her time unbuttoning his shirt and pulling his T-shirt over his head.

She roamed her fingers across his chest, loving the feel of his muscles dancing beneath her touch.

"You're good at this," he praised.

"I'm a fast learner." She winked and reached for his belt buckle.

Their eyes locked when it came time for her to unbutton his pants. He looked as if he wanted to see how far she would go and she was eager to show him.

"A boxer man, huh?"

He drew her close again. "I hope that doesn't disappoint you."

"Not at all." His bare chest felt wonderful against her.

"Good." He whispered her name before kissing her again, then moved lower. With skilled hands, he unfastened her bra and moaned his appreciation when he freed her breasts.

Cool air and warm breath swirled over her nipples. His tongue danced over one peak and then he nipped at the other with his teeth. Leila rolled her head back and thrust her breasts as high she could get them. He rewarded her efforts by cupping both breasts and increasing the pressure of his suckling.

This was heaven.

Garrick released his hold and tugged at her panties. A second later, they, too, fell to her feet. He reclaimed her mouth, but stole her breath when his hard shaft branded her thigh.

Leila quivered as he backed her up against the cold bricks of the fireplace. She winced with pain and pleasure and then she heard the unmistakable rip of a condom packet.

He lifted her right leg and placed it around his

hip, then gently reached for the other, supporting her weight with the greatest of ease.

Leila's heartbeat was beyond erratic as he glided inside, filling her inch by inch. She dug her fingernails across his back, down his waist, and across his buttocks as they moved together.

Garrick's sweet murmurings filled her head as he rocked her to new dizzying heights. She needed this; she needed him like no man before. She didn't know when she'd started saying his name; all she knew was she couldn't stop.

"Leila. Sweet Leila."

His husky whisper finally pitched her over the edge and she released a low cry of release.

Garrick slowed, allowing her body to quake with several aftershocks. He rained kisses over her face, down her neck, and then once again over her breasts.

When her breathing finally returned to normal, he clasped his arms around her waist and showed remarkable strength as he carried her over to the blanket. Once there, he gave her butt a quick smack.

"Lay down," he commanded.

Still eager and willing to please, Leila untwined her legs from around his hips and eased down onto the blanket. At this new angle, she was blown away at the sheer beauty of his chocolate body.

Garrick slid down beside her and tilted her chin up so he could gaze into her eyes. "How are you feeling?" The pad of his fingers rubbed her hard nipples.

"Wonderful," she admitted.

He waited, and she sensed that he wanted her to take control for a while. Happy to oblige, Leila reached between his legs and stroked his rock-hard shaft.

Garrick smiled and leaned forward to steal another kiss.

She placed her free hand against his chest. "Lay back," she said.

His lips slid wider as he did as she asked.

Leila climbed to her knees, and then swung one leg over and straddled him for the top position. She emitted a long catlike purr as she eased down on him and found her own rhythm.

After a long while, Leila's breath hitched and her body stiffened as a swirling heat built inside of her. She dropped her head back as her rhythm increased in urgency.

Garrick's hands fell to her hips while his own religious moans fell from his lips. They moved in unison, their hips rocking in unbelievable intensity.

Leila's climax slammed into her and paralyzed her vocal cords. Garrick quickly rolled her onto her back and rocked hard and steady until he cried out her name in one last powerful thrust.

At long last, he collapsed on top of her. They lay melded together, heaving for air.

"You're amazing," he said, finding the strength to rain kisses along her collarbone.

"You're not so bad yourself." She pushed him onto his side, but didn't separate their bodies. "I hope you had some spinach tonight. You're going to need your energy."

"Trash talking in bed. That's unique," he laughed.

"If you haven't noticed, we're not in bed."

"Yet." He winked.

Leila gasped at the feel of his sex hardening inside of her. "You're ready for round two so soon?"

"Honey, I'm just getting started." He pulled her close, and then proved that he was a man of his word.

Chapter 15

Leila woke with a smile on her face as she uncurled her body in a long feline stretch. She couldn't remember the last time she'd slept so well. It had to have been at least—a week ago.

She loved the way her body tingled and how her mind still lolled among the clouds. Had she ever felt this way before? Her lips slid wider as she rolled her body back into a fetal position.

She drew in a deep breath, catching a whiff of his cologne in her feather pillows. *How would*

Garrick aka "Mr. All Night" feel about making love in the morning?

Leila stretched out her hand to find out; but her dreamworld shattered when she discovered the spot next to her empty.

Her eyes bolted open as she jerked up in bed. "Garrick?" She glanced around, and sure enough, the room was empty. "What the…?"

Had last night been a dream?

She peeled back the sheets and cool air sent an army of goose bumps charging throughout her body. There was only one reason why Leila would go to bed nude, which meant last night couldn't have been a dream.

Quickly, she detangled herself from her tousled sheets and rushed to put on her robe. All the while, she had a horrifying thought of Garrick treating last night as a wham-bam-thank-you-ma'am, which was usually her role.

Humiliation flushed through her body as she tore out of her bedroom and stormed down the hall.

"I see you're finally up."

Garrick's warm baritone stopped her cold before the baby's room. She turned toward the open door, stunned to see him in the rocking chair, feeding Emma her morning bottle.

She exhaled with relief and fluttered an embarrassed smile at him. "How long have you been up?" she asked, seeing him dressed in his pants and T-shirt.

"About an hour when this little lady started bawling for breakfast."

"Oh, why didn't you wake me?" she moaned and raked her hands through her hair. "I would have fed her."

Garrick shrugged. "You looked so peaceful…and I figured that since I had a hand in that, I should be the one to take care of the baby."

Leila grew warm as a familiar ache throbbed between her legs.

"I tried to feed Emma some oatmeal, but it seems to me she was more interested in wearing it than eating it." He chuckled, winking at her niece.

She laughed. "Been there, done that." Leila folded her arms and leaned against the door frame, fascinated by the sight of him with Emma.

"You really do love children, don't you?" she asked suddenly.

"What's not to love?" He glanced up and met her stare. "Children are an extension of ourselves—a little piece of immortality. Plus, they're so darn cute." He winked.

Touched, Leila's heart squeezed with sadness. Slowly, reality drizzled and then flooded her brain. She and Garrick were polar opposites in every way and yet last night…

"Is something wrong?"

She tried to shake off her troubled thoughts, but the enormity of what had transpired between them continued to seep into her brain.

"Leila?"

Once again, their eyes met and she forced on a brave smile. "I think you'll make a wonderful father one day," she admitted. He frowned; but she turned away.

"Where are you going?"

To go sulk in a corner. "I'm going to make some coffee. Would you like some?"

Garrick stared back, wondering if he'd said something wrong. His lips constricted as he waited, studying her. "Coffee would be nice."

Leila tightened the belt on her robe and strolled from the doorway.

Emma's small hand grabbed the neck of Garrick's T-shirt and returned his attention to the gurgling and cooing baby. He removed the bottle from her mouth.

"Are all the women in your family this difficult?"

The baby clapped her hands over her eyes and gave him a wonderful belly laugh.

"I'm going to take that as a yes." He reached out for a burp cloth and swung it over his shoulder.

As he descended the stairs, he bounced and patted Emma's back. However, he was unprepared to find Leila next to the coffeemaker, sobbing.

"Leila?"

Her head jerked up and, upon seeing him, she backhanded her tears. "Oh, um. I didn't hear you come down." She attempted to smile. "How would you like your coffee?"

Garrick strolled across the kitchen and settled Emma into her high chair before he faced Leila. "Tell me what's wrong," he urged, wiping a few missed tears with his fingers.

"Nothing," she lied, trying to quell the embarrassment and panic mushrooming inside of her.

"Surely, you don't think I buy that, do you?" He slid his arm around her waist and pulled her forward.

"Don't." Leila placed her hands against his chest and gained some distance—even if it was just a few inches.

He didn't push, but he didn't release her either. "I'm pretty stubborn, too, you know. I can stand like this all day."

An awkward chuckle tumbled from her, yet she couldn't quite bring herself to look him in the eye.

"What is it, Leila?" he whispered, and then peppered kisses against her forehead and temples.

Why did he have to be so wonderful? "I think last night was a mistake," she croaked, the words sour on her tongue.

His hold loosened, but didn't surrender. "I don't," he said.

"You will." She closed her eyes, but a few tears managed to escape their confines.

"Why don't you let me be the judge of that?"

When he laughed, Leila caught the slight

titter of nervousness. Leila feigned bravado and lifted her chin in order to meet his eyes. "I'm not what you want—or need. I'm a career woman, through and through. I'm not going to apologize for it. I'm married to my job…and I don't see children in my future."

He was no longer smiling. "But you have little Emma—"

"Until tomorrow. My sister Roslyn will be back from Barbados and she's agreed to take Emma."

Garrick's arms fell to his sides as he spoke resolutely, "I see."

Suddenly the distance between them seemed wider than a mere few inches.

"Last night," she continued in a shaky whisper, "was wonderful."

"But it was still a mistake?"

She nodded and then dropped her head, unable to bear the look of hurt in his eyes.

They fell silent with only Emma's soft cooing in the background.

After a long while, Garrick reached for her hand. "What if I said that I didn't care?" he asked.

Leila glanced up questioningly.

"What if I said that I didn't care if you didn't want children?"

Her lips quivered into a smile. "Then I'd know you were lying." She removed her hands from his grasp. "Let's just say that last night was a one-time thing and let it go."

Muscles twitched along Garrick's jawline as he finally dropped his gaze. "All right." He stepped back and drew in a breath.

"I hope this doesn't mean that we can't still be friends," she added.

Garrick said nothing but turned and strolled over to Emma. "Bye, sweetheart." He leaned down and kissed the baby's upturned cheek.

When he walked away, Emma's wide eyes followed him out of the kitchen. Once he was out of sight, the baby scrunched up her face and began to cry.

Leila rushed over and picked up her niece. "It's okay." She bounced the child in her arms. "I know exactly how you feel."

Even though she left a part of her heart in beautiful Barbados, the moment Roslyn and her family touched down at Atlanta Hartsfield-

Jackson airport, she was glad to be home again. Not to mention that her heart raced at the mere thought of having another baby in the house.

Patrick and the children also couldn't contain their excitement. Upon returning home, everyone pitched in to turn the home office into something suitable for Emma.

"You're not pregnant, but you're glowing," Patrick observed as his wife ushered into the room carrying piles of old baby paraphernalia.

"What can I say? I'm happy."

He nodded, but turned thoughtful as she continued to organize the room. "Has, uh, Leila heard anything from Samantha yet?"

Roslyn's hands slowed as she folded blankets. "Not yet. She really hasn't had the time to really look for her."

"You know…Samantha never really stays gone for long."

The statement hung between them for a time before she finally glanced over at him. "What are you saying?"

He sighed as his shoulders slumped. "You know what I'm saying. Sooner or later Sam is going to come back."

Roslyn shrugged. "It doesn't mean that she's going to want a child."

"She already has a child." He moved over to stand next to his wife. "I just don't want to see you get hurt."

"You mean that you don't want me to get too attached to the baby."

"I know it's going to be hard—"

"It's going to be impossible," Roslyn corrected.

Patrick nodded. "It will be for all of us. I'm equally worried about how this will impact our girls."

Tears crested her eyes, but she mopped them with her hands before they had a chance to fall. "It's not her fault, you know?"

He said nothing.

"Momma did this to Sam," Roslyn offered as an excuse. "Mom's suicide was the hardest on her. She never got over that somehow it was her fault. I think each of us believes that we had something to do with it. If we were better children, she wouldn't have left. You know, that sort of thing."

"It's not true." He drew her into his arms.

"I know, but Sam—"

"I'm not judging Sam," he said. "But we all have these horrible demons to fight for one reason or another. Sooner or later Sam is going to have to *fight* her own. Not you—not Leila. If not for her sake, for Emma's."

More tears splashed down Roslyn's face. "I know you're right."

The phone rang and Courtney raced through the hall. "I'll get it!"

Roslyn and Patrick smiled and broke apart. "Okay, I'll promise not to get *too* attached to Emma staying here."

"That's all I'm asking." He leaned over and kissed her. "Now, I better get up to the attic and get some more of those boxes."

"Daddy, Daddy," Courtney said, rushing into the room. "Telephone."

Patrick rolled his eyes as he headed over to the cordless. "I guess the world knows we're back home."

"We had to come out of hiding some time," Roslyn joked, drying her eyes.

"Hello."

"Yes. Mr. Sanders? This is Dr. Benjamin Ray. I'm calling about your father."

Chapter 16

Leila moved methodically around the baby room, packing everything she'd bought in the last seven days. The task proved harder than she'd expected, but it was one she was determined to get through.

Emma watched her from the playpen as she crisscrossed the room.

"Trust me. You're going to love living at your aunt Roslyn's," Leila promised. "You'll have your uncle Patrick and your cousins Courtney and Breanna to play with."

"Aaah!" Emma shouted, clapping her hands.

In the last twenty-four hours, the child seemed to really enjoy the sound of her own voice.

Leila smiled and resumed what she was doing. One thing was for sure, she could finally get back to her job. She still needed to hunt for a new distributor. The magazine's next issue was due to go to press in the next week—and of course there was still the issue of searching for Sam.

She sighed. In the chaos, Sam had slipped Leila's mind. She hoped her sister was okay—prayed that she didn't do something stupid—again. After so many years, it was hard to deal with someone who made it a point to emotionally hijack Leila every time she came around.

"Now, don't think this is going to be the last time you see me," Leila told Emma. "I'm going to visit you at Roslyn's every chance I get."

"Aaah!" Emma grabbed her plastic keys and jiggled them around.

Leila's heart melted as she cast another sidelong glance at the child.

Children are an extension of ourselves—a little piece of immortality.

She cocked her head and could clearly see Samantha and even Nicole.

"Aaah!" Emma jiggled the keys again.

Leila blinked out of her reverie just as the phone rang. "I bet I know who that is," she said excitedly, and then extracted Emma from her pen. "Let's go see if that's Aunt Roslyn."

She rushed down the hall and picked up the extension in her bedroom. "Hello."

"Leila?"

"Hey, Ros. I told Emma it was you."

An awkward pause filtered over the line before Leila caught the faint sound of a sniffle. "Is everything all right?"

"Actually, no," her sister admitted. "There's been a change of plans. We just received a call from a hospital in Boston."

"Hospital?" Leila's pulse leaped. "It's not Sam?"

"No. It's Patrick's father. He's suffered a massive stroke and he's in a coma." Roslyn sniffed. "We're going to fly out there tonight."

"Tonight?" Leila blinked, and then glanced down at Emma. "So that means—?"

"I'm not going to be able to take Emma until we get back. Is that going to be all right?"

A strange mixture of relief and anxiety

rushed through her. "Yes. Yes, of course. How is Patrick holding up?"

"Fine so far, but…" Roslyn lowered her voice. "You know how close he is with his father."

Leila bobbed her head and then remembered her sister couldn't see her. "Yes, I know. Tell him I'm sorry and I'll keep his father in my prayers."

"I will. Kiss little Emma for me and I'll see you both when we return."

Leila said her goodbyes and then returned the phone to its cradle. Now what was she going to do?

"Aaah! Aaah!" Emma banged her keys against Leila's head.

"Ow. Do you mind?"

Her niece giggled, and then shoved the keys into her mouth.

"I'm so glad I amuse you. 'Cause it looks like you're stuck with me for a little while longer. God help us."

Garrick's first day back to work was hectic at best and chaotic at worst. Yet, he didn't mind it a bit. He welcomed anything that would keep his mind off Leila Owens.

Ned Griffin, Garrick's right-hand man, breezed into his office. "There's a delay with the Reynolds project out in Buckhead."

Garrick leaned forward and steepled his hands beneath his chin. "What is it now?"

"Foreman says the measurements are wrong."

"My measurements are never wrong," Garrick boasted with a cocksure smile. "Who's the foreman?"

"Arquette," Ned said.

Garrick huffed. "Arquette is always complaining about the measurements and every time he's wrong. How does this clown keep finding work?"

"He has a lot of friends. You want to give him a call or should I?"

"I'll do it." Garrick snatched up the phone, but halted when he heard a knock at the door. He glanced up, stunned to see Miranda standing in his doorway, swollen belly and all.

"Hi. Can I come in?" she asked.

Ned glanced from the doorway and then to his boss. "I'll come back later."

Miranda smiled as she sidestepped and allowed Ned to pass.

"Good seeing you again, Miranda."

"You, too, Ned."

Garrick rolled his eyes and returned the phone to his desk.

Miranda hovered near the doorway. "You didn't answer my question."

"Sure. It's a free country."

Miranda hesitated, and then entered the room. "I came by to give you this." She handed over a thick envelope.

"What is it?"

"The house sold," she said. "That's your half of the money." She lowered her hands and fidgeted.

"You didn't have to bring this over. That's what lawyers are for." He smirked.

Miranda burst into tears.

Stunned, Garrick blinked. When his brain kicked into gear he rushed around his desk. "I'm sorry. I was joking," he comforted her awkwardly. "I didn't mean to upset you."

"It's all right. It's just this pregnancy." She fumbled and withdrew a tissue from her purse. "I cry all the time now."

"Oh." He relaxed and stepped back. "You

scared me for a moment there. I thought something was wrong."

"Oh, no. It's just…" She twisted her face as she burst into more tears. "He left me!"

"What?" He directed her over to a chair.

"Mark left me." She sniffed. "He said that everything was moving too fast and that he wasn't sure he was ready to become a father. Ready. Can you believe that? He's forty-nine years old!"

Lost for words, Garrick could do no more than stare at her. What was he supposed to say?

Miranda quickly drenched her tissue and dug through her purse for another. "I should have known better. Mark was never like you—kind, patient, and adored children."

Garrick's hackles stood at attention. She was going somewhere with this. "*We* were a long time ago."

"I made a mistake." She clutched his hand. "It was a *big* mistake. Can you ever forgive me?"

Garrick fingered his tie loose as the room grew scorching hot. "Miranda, there's nothing to forgive. We were simply two people who wanted different things out of a marriage. It was what you would call a no-fault divorce. I don't blame you."

"That's not true." She shook her head vigorously. "I do want the same things. I want the house and the children and the picket fence."

Garrick glanced down at her protruding belly.

Miranda tilted his chin up to meet her shimmering eyes. "I have to know. Is there any way you can give me a second chance?"

Chapter 17

As January melted into February, Leila's life continued to change. After the Alison fiasco, she had given up the notion of finding a sitter or nanny for Emma. Instead, she hired movers and had Ciara and her office moved to her residence.

In retrospect, she didn't know why she hadn't thought of this solution before. Staff meetings were held during Emma's naps and by video teleconference; same-day carriers delivered photo layouts, art direction proposals, and articles.

"You are my idol." Ciara breezed over to her desk and handed Leila her afternoon coffee and Emma's juice bottle. "I should have known you would figure out a way to run a magazine and be a full-time mom."

"A full-time aunt," Leila corrected while she played patty-cake with Emma.

"C'mon. You can't tell me that you're not enjoying yourself. You should see how you light up every time this little cutie is around." Ciara bent down and pinched Emma's chubby cheeks.

Emma giggled, prominently showing off her two bottom teeth.

"You know, it's not too late for you to have one yourself," Ciara said, patting her barely there bulge.

"So you keep telling me." Leila rolled her eyes. "And I keep telling you it's never going to happen."

Ciara shrugged. "I know I can't wait to have a little Elmo running around the house."

"Heck, I can buy you one of those," Leila joked.

"Ha. Ha."

"What can I say? You walked right into that one."

The phone rang and Ciara stretched across Leila's desk to answer. "Leila Owens's office."

Leila settled her niece on her lap and fed her the juice bottle.

"Yes, just a moment." Ciara placed a hand across the mouthpiece and whispered, "It's Mr. Porter with Hearst."

Irritated, Leila weighed whether she should take the call and then decided that it was just best to get the damn thing over with.

"Here, I'll take her." Ciara reached for Emma while Leila grabbed the phone.

"Mr. Porter, how nice to hear from you again."

Every week Leila and Mr. Porter had the same conversation. Hearst would increase their offer and she would turn it down. Lately, it was getting harder to do so.

"I still think you're crazy," Ciara said in between blowing raspberries on Emma's chest. "There's no way I would turn down—how much are they up to now?"

"Eighty-two million."

Ciara clasped a hand to her throat and pretended to choke. "Great Scott. You really have flipped."

"Great Scott?"

"No cursing around the kid, remember?"

The small reminder was enough to send Leila's thoughts careening toward Garrick. In the past month, she'd practically put herself under house arrest to avoid running into him.

The whole thing was silly. The lifespan of their relationship had only lasted a week. However, it didn't explain her constantly peering through windows and hoping to catch a glimpse of him.

So far, she'd learned his bedroom light clicked on at five-thirty every weekday morning and eight o'clock on the weekends. When going to work, he dressed impeccably in a suit and tie and was out the door by 7:00 a.m.; and he was home no later than 7:00 p.m.

Fleetingly, she wondered if her actions constituted stalking, but she dismissed them as harmless curiosity. There was nothing wrong with checking to see how he was doing.

"Never mind. I see you're zoning out on me again."

Ciara's words snapped Leila from her thoughts. "I'm sorry. What were you saying?"

"Apparently nothing you want to hear." Ciara stood and placed Emma in her playpen. "If we're going to continue to work this close together, you're going to have to work on your conversational skills."

"You got it." Leila saluted and then resumed poring over paperwork. "Did Jeannie ever fax or e-mail her feature story?"

"Oh." Ciara snapped her fingers. "I picked it up when I swung by the office this morning. I must have left it in my car. Since I've gotten pregnant, my memory has been shot."

"Put that on your list of things *not* to admit to your boss."

"If you ever get pregnant, you'll see what I mean," Ciara said over her shoulder as she headed toward the front door.

She was still smiling when she stepped out of the house and walked over to her car. As she opened her passenger-side door, a car pulled into the driveway across the street. At long last, she was going to actually catch a peek at her boss's good-looking neighbor.

Whatever she'd expected, it wasn't the six-foot-plus brother with the body of a gladiator.

He was dressed in a pair of sweatpants and a T-shirt, and when he bent over to grab something from the trunk, Ciara swore she could bounce a quarter off his tight butt.

"Now *that's* fine." She snatched up Jeannie's feature story, smiled, and then whistled on her way back to the house.

"What are you so happy about?" Leila asked.

Ciara plopped the story down on Leila's desk. "The sight of a good-looking man tends to do that to me—and the one across the street is above grade-A quality. Girl, you weren't lying about him."

"Garrick." Leila started to jump up from her chair, but caught herself. "He's all right." Leila dropped her gaze to read Jeannie's story.

"All right?" Ciara thundered. "That's not what you told me five weeks ago. You said, 'gorgeous doesn't do him justice.'"

"I thought you couldn't remember anything?"

"I'm not going to forget his fine butt. Speaking of which, did you see it?"

"Oh, yeah. I saw all right." Leila flipped to the second page of the article despite not reading a single word. However, she did have a perfect image of Garrick's naked butt in her head—and a smile on her face.

Ciara cocked her head. "What is that supposed to mean? Why are you smiling?"

"Hmmm?" Leila pretended she hadn't heard the question.

"Did you and your neighbor…hook up or something?"

"What?" Leila overplayed her reaction and could see Ciara didn't buy it.

"You did, didn't you?" she screamed and jumped up and down. "When? Where? Why didn't you tell me? Are you going to see him again?"

Groaning, Leila rolled her eyes and dropped the charade. "Calm down. It's no big deal."

"No big deal, are you kidding me?" Ciara stopped cheerleading. "Don't tell me. He was lousy in bed." She slapped her arms to her sides. "I should have known something that fine would have a fault."

Leila laughed. "No. He wasn't lousy."

"Really?" Ciara gasped. "Then how good was he?"

"I'm not going to discuss this with you."

"Oh, that good?" Ciara grabbed a chair and pulled it up to Leila. "I want details."

Leila's laughter quickly dissipated. "There's nothing to tell."

"You mean that you don't want to tell me."

"That, too."

Ciara slumped back hard against her chair and folded her arms like a child denied her favorite candy.

Leila tried to refocus her attention on the article, but could feel Ciara's heavy gaze follow her.

"He's a dog, isn't he?" Ciara guessed. "He seduced you and then did the old hit-and-run routine."

"No. That's not what happened either." Leila sighed. "Garrick is a wonderful man… and I wouldn't wish me on him for nothing in the world."

"What is that supposed to mean?"

"Nothing. Forget about it."

Ciara didn't move.

"And will you stop that?" Leila snapped.

"Stop what?"

"Staring at me! Don't you have some work to

do or am I paying you just to keep me company?"

Ciara blinked at her, and then finally climbed up from the chair. "Sorry, Ms. Owens. I didn't mean to intrude." She paused, and then added, "It's just that I thought we were friends, too. I won't make the mistake again."

She turned and crossed the room to her desk.

Once again, Leila felt like an ass. "Ciara, I'm sorry. I didn't mean it that way."

Her secretary kept her back toward her. "In what way did you mean it?"

"C'mon. Don't do this. Of course, we're friends. It's just that…I just made a mistake with Garrick, that's all."

Ciara turned around. "I'm listening."

Now she had to tell the whole damn story, which contradicted her desire to just forget about Garrick. However, as she started talking about her New Year's rendezvous, her blood warmed and she could hardly sit still.

"Let me make sure I understand this," Ciara said when Leila finished. "You dumped him?"

"We're totally wrong for each other. It was best to end it before anything got started."

"Something had already started," she reminded her.

"We want different things."

"Sounds to me like you wanted each other."

"See, this is why I didn't tell you." Leila shoved the feature article into her in-box to look at later. "You're always reading more into things."

"Me? That sounds like you."

"That's not true." Leila frowned and folded her arms defensively.

"Yes, it is. Every time you get remotely interested in someone, you drag out more baggage than a 757 can carry. This one doesn't have a good job, that one is a lousy kisser, and XYZ isn't an intellectual. Now Mr. Fine across the street, who has a good damn job, and can do the *New York Times* crossword puzzle, and can make your toes *curl* during sex actually has the nerve to want to settle down and have children. Let me get out my violin so I can play you a sad tune."

"Very funny."

"No, it's not." Ciara grew serious. "You have to stop pushing people away. Humans are designed to cohabit. We long for companionship and you are no different. You just like to pretend you are."

Leila vehemently denied Ciara's words long after she'd gone home for the evening. Leila didn't push people away. That was Samantha—not her. She had plenty of friends and just because she tended to engage in no-strings-attached types of relationships didn't mean that she had intimacy issues.

"What do you think?" she asked Emma as she fed her dinner in her high chair.

"Aaah! Baah!" Emma smacked her hands on the tray.

Leila had learned how to maneuver around flailing arms and grabby fingers, and didn't miss an inch shoveling in the next scoop of baby food. "I knew you would agree with me. Just because I don't want to date Garrick doesn't mean that there's something *wrong* with me. So what if he's gorgeous?"

Emma cocked her head and batted her long curly lashes at her.

"Oh, so you're going to turn on me, too. That's just great." Leila spooned in the last of the creamed peas when the doorbell rang. "Were you expecting someone?"

"Aaah. Baah!"

"Me, neither." She wiped her niece's mouth, swooped her out of the chair, and went to answer the door.

"Roslyn!" Leila blinked. "You're back." She reached out and enclosed her sister in a one-arm embrace. "It seems like forever since I've seen you. Come in. Come in."

"Is this little Emma?" Roslyn pinched the baby's cheeks as she crossed the threshold. "She looks so much like Samantha."

"I know. It's eerie, isn't it?" Leila closed the door while a sliver of anxiety snaked through her. "I wasn't expecting you tonight."

"I know. The girls and I came back early. Courtney has missed enough school. I don't want her to have to repeat the first grade."

"How's Patrick's father?"

"Still in a coma," she relayed sadly. "It's pretty much a waiting game. The doctors are skeptical on whether he's going to pull through."

"I'm so sorry. How's your husband holding up?"

"Status quo." She shrugged. "About as good as expected. And how are you two holding up?" She caressed Emma's cheek with open longing.

"We're doing great!" Leila said, perking up. "We just finished up dinner. Next is bath time and then bedtime."

Roslyn's eyebrows rose as she shifted her gaze to Leila.

"What?"

"What? You. Ms. Mommy. And here I was worried about you. Seems you have this whole baby thing down pat."

Leila relaxed as she led the way to the living room. "Are you thirsty? Can I get you anything to drink?"

"No. I'm fine." Roslyn settled on the sofa and looked up at them. "Can I hold her?"

"Uh, sure." Leila glanced down at her niece before she reluctantly passed her to Roslyn.

Her sister was instantly enamored with her niece. Jealousy entwined with Leila's anxiety. Had Roslyn come to take Emma home with her?

Leila sat across from the sofa in an easy chair and watched the two bond together. Her mind raced with excuses as to why Emma couldn't leave tonight—with each one she worried whether it was good enough. Would Roslyn fight her on it?

"Would you like to come and stay with me?" Roslyn asked, bouncing Emma on her knee. "Would you like that? Would ya?"

"Uhm." Leila cleared her throat and fidgeted with her hands.

Roslyn looked over at her. "Is something wrong?"

"No, nothing's wrong." Leila licked her lips. "There's just been a slight change in plans."

"Oh?"

"Yeah. See." Leila drew a deep breath. "I want to keep Emma."

Chapter 18

"Honey, why do you keep peeking out of the window at that house?" Miranda asked, joining Garrick in the dining room. "Is something wrong?"

"No. I've never seen that car over there before," he said, trying to make out the license plate. "I wonder who it is?" he added under his breath.

"Why don't you go talk to her? You're apparently crazy about the woman…or would you rather I pass a note to her? If you like Garrick, please check yes or no," she said and laughed.

"Very funny." He pulled away from the window and returned to the table. "It's a little more complicated than that."

"No more complicated than getting me and Mark back together." She stretched out a hand to clasp his. "Which I can never thank you enough for."

He smiled and shook his head. "It was just a bad case of wedding jitters. A lot of men go through it."

"Did you?"

Garrick's lips sloped unevenly as he contemplated his answer.

"On second thought, don't answer that." She gathered the plates off the table.

"Hey, you don't have to do that. You cooked, I'll clean up."

"Dinner was my thank-you gift. For helping Mark and I…and for you laughing me out of your office that day I asked you to take me back."

"You have to admit it was pretty funny." He stood and took the plates out of her hands. "We were a bad match from the beginning. The bad part is I think we knew it all along. You hid behind your job while I thought if we started a family it would fix everything."

"It would have made things worse."

"I know that now."

"But, hey. As crazy as this may sound, I still think you'll make a wonderful father some day."

"This is really a warped conversation. You know that, right?"

"Yeah," she agreed. "But I'm glad we're friends now."

He nodded, enjoying the weight lifted from his shoulders. "Me, too."

The doorbell rang just as he headed off to the kitchen.

"I'll get it," Miranda offered, waddling off toward the front door. "It's probably Mark. I paged him about a half hour ago." She opened the door, prepared to swing her arms around her fiancé, but stopped short when her brain registered the attractive woman from across the street.

Stunned, Leila's smile froze on her face, while her eyes traveled over the very beautiful and very *pregnant* woman.

"Oh, hello," the woman said.

"Who is it, Miranda?" Garrick's voice boomed from somewhere in the house.

Miranda—the ex-wife? Leila jerked out of her trance as her grip tightened on the baby-monitor receiver. "I'm sorry. I didn't mean to disturb you." She turned.

"No, wait," the woman called after her.

Leila bolted. No way was she going to stick around to make a fool out of herself. She stepped out in the street and heard the screech of tires. Turning, she placed her hands out, dropping the monitor and her house keys on the hood of a car.

"Hey, watch where you're going," the driver yelled out the side of his car.

"Leila!"

Heart pounding, she glanced back at Garrick's place to see him race through the door. Quickly, she grabbed her things and ran to her house.

"Leila, wait."

What had she hoped to accomplish by showing up at his door this time of night? Did she honestly think telling him that she was keeping Emma was going to change anything? "I'm such a fool." She reached the door, slid the key into the lock; but she'd only gotten one foot through the door when Garrick's strong fingers clamped around her arm.

"Let go of me," she shouted, snatching her arm.

"It's not what you think," he said, ignoring the order.

"I'm not thinking anything," she lied, still struggling for freedom.

"Then why did you run away?" he barked.

She couldn't think of an answer, but fought him all the same. "Just go away."

"Not until you answer me," he hissed and pushed her through the door, his grip still firm.

"What are you doing?" she asked in startled alarm.

He kicked the door shut with the back of his heel. "I'm talking to you."

"There's nothing to talk about. So why don't you just go back home to your *wife*."

"My *ex*-wife," he corrected. The corners of his lips curled upward. "I think I told you that before."

"You also told me that you were no longer on

speaking terms and that she was not interested in motherhood. Looks like all that was a lie."

"Things change." He released her.

At his words, tears stung the backs of her eyes.

"Is there a problem?" Roslyn's voice floated from upstairs.

Garrick and Leila sprang apart.

"No." She cleared her throat and fluttered a smile at her sister. "We were just…talking."

Slowly, Roslyn descended the staircase. "Talking pretty loudly. You could have awakened the baby." Her eyes fastened on Garrick as she stopped in front of him. "I'm Roslyn. Leila's sister." She extended her hand.

He politely accepted it. "Garrick Grayson. I'm trying to date your neurotic sister."

"What?" Leila rounded on him. "You were just with…you can't just blab that out to her!"

"Why not?"

"Pleased to meet you," Roslyn butted in, and then winked at her sister. "I'm going to go ahead and go now. Emma is asleep. Are you sure you're all right?"

Jaws clenched, Leila nodded.

"All right then." Roslyn settled her purse strap on her shoulder, bent down to pick up the child monitor, and handed it back to Leila. "I'll let you two finish your conversation." She opened the door. "Walk me to the car, Leila?"

Leila tilted up her chin, shoved the monitor in his hands, and stepped around him. "Listen out for the baby."

"Yes, ma'am."

She rolled her eyes and followed her sister out the door. The minute they were alone, her mind crowded with explanations to tell her sister. "Look, about what happened in there."

Roslyn reached her car and turned with her hands pressed against her mouth.

It took Leila a moment to realize that her sister was actually laughing.

"What's so funny?"

"You. Him." Roslyn's shoulders quaked as her laughter filled the night air. "I couldn't have dreamed of a better match."

"You just met him."

"True, but he obviously knows how to handle you—that alone is impressive. Plus, I think he cares a lot for you." She walked over to Leila and threw her arms around her. "And something tells me that you feel the same way about him."

Denial crested Leila's tongue but never fell from her lips.

"Call me in the morning to tell me how it went. I'd love to have some good news." Roslyn got into her car and waved as she pulled out of the driveway.

Across the street, Garrick's ex-wife waddled out with her arm entwined with a tall, handsome stranger. After he opened the car door for her, he took Miranda in his arms and delivered a long kiss before helping her into the car.

"I wish someone would just stamp the word *ass* on my forehead and just get it over with," Leila mumbled under her breath and then slunk back toward the house.

Garrick waited for her in the foyer. "I like your sister."

Leila shut the door behind her. "She seems to like you, too." An awkward silence flowed between them. "Look, about what happened earlier—"

"Yes?"

"I—I, uhm, I might owe you an apology."

"Might?"

"Yes." She shifted nervously on her feet. "I *might* have overreacted…when I saw you with your ex-wife."

Garrick crossed his arms. "Uh-huh."

"It's just when I saw her…and then I saw you…"

"Yes?"

"You're not making this easy." She dropped her arms at her sides. "You could let me off the hook here."

"I'm waiting for you to admit it."

Leila grew uneasy. "Admit what?"

He walked over to her. "That you were jealous."

"Don't be ridiculous." She rolled her eyes and shied away. However, his soft chuckle told her he hadn't bought the act.

"You're a beautiful liar." He placed his finger beneath her chin and forced her to meet his gaze. "You're also *my* beautiful liar." He gathered her into his arms and absorbed her body heat.

Before Leila could draw a breath, he captured her lips in a long exploratory kiss. Time either melted away or stood still, Leila couldn't tell which. She only knew the taste of him was the sweetest homecoming she'd ever known.

Mindless, she fumbled with his shirt buttons until he took control and snapped them open with a forceful jerk. He broke the kiss just long enough to pull his T-shirt off in one fluid swish.

A groan escaped his throat as their lips reunited. Slowly, deliberately, he slid his body against hers and elicited a submissive moan. "You know. You never did tell me why you came over to see me," he whispered, and then resumed kissing.

"Huh—what?"

"Why did you come to see me? Was it for more of this?" He eased back a bit and snatched her shirt over her head. Tonight's lingerie was good ol' fashioned U.S.A. cotton.

"Sorry. No silk or lace tonight."

"No apologies needed. It's still getting the job done. Trust me on that."

His strong hands glided up her toned abs and slid beneath the elastic band of her bra. Leila gasped, but then tried to will her pulse to slow down. She didn't want to rush. She wanted to savor every moment so she would have it branded forever in her memory.

No matter what she did, she had no control over her body, heart, or mind. He ruled over everything and by the time her panties hit the floor, she no longer cared.

"I'm still waiting for you to answer my question." He propped her up against the foyer table.

Leila blinked and tried to think. "Uh, it's not important."

"Sure it is." He slid a hand into her as his mouth closed around a jutted nipple.

Everything turned into a kaleidoscope of color behind her eyelids as she gave into the feeling of free-falling into an unknown abyss. At first, his hand's slow measured rhythm felt as if he were caressing her soul; but as the tempo accelerated, and she could hardly catch her breath, she felt like a woman dancing on top of hot coals—and loving every minute of it.

Her hips joined in on the dance, just as Garrick exchanged one oversensitive breast for the other. At the feel of her first orgasm surfacing, Leila's breathing became shallow and a cry clogged in her throat.

She slammed her head back against the wall at the force of her release, but she didn't care. She was ready for more.

Willing to oblige, Garrick selected a few more positions that became instant favorites for Leila. After each one, her appetite for him only grew. With a few intermittent breaks, the night soon morphed into morning. Soon after, Emma's cry for breakfast came just as exhaustion kicked in.

Garrick lifted his head off the staircase. "Your turn to get the baby."

Chapter 19

As it turned out, Emma wasn't quite ready for breakfast and had fallen back to sleep almost as soon as Leila had entered the room. Thankful for the reprieve, she quickly joined Garrick in her bedroom.

His eyes fluttered open and a smile hooked his lips the moment she slid beneath the sheets. Both lay on their bellies while they faced one another.

"You know I'm still waiting, don't you?"

She frowned and then her brain kicked into gear. "Oh, why did I come over?"

He nodded and scooted closer. "You didn't think I forgot, did you?"

"If you want me to remember, you need to keep your distance." She laughed as she snuggled against her pillow. "You tend to have a strange effect on me."

"And here I thought that was a good thing."

She twitched and scooted closer herself. "It's definitely a good thing."

"What are you—the Energizer Bunny?"

"Complaints from the peanut gallery?"

"Not at all." He lifted his head and leaned over for a smooch. "So about your visit last night?"

Leila sighed. "It's no big deal really. I just came over…to tell you about my decision to keep Emma." She blinked. It sounded silly now that the words were out of her mouth, but the truth was the moment she'd told Roslyn of her decision, she'd been stunned that she'd changed her mind about motherhood and that it had happened with a snap of her finger.

"You're going to raise Emma?" Garrick questioned, reshaping his pillow. "Are you sure about this? It's a big step."

"I know," she admitted with a warm but lazy

smile. "But it feels right, you know? When Roslyn showed up last night, I—I was just filled with this anxiety and this fierce possessiveness that I just blurted it out."

Garrick's smile grew. "How do you feel now?"

She paused and gave serious thought to the question and her answer. "Good. I feel like I made the right decision."

"So you're going to balance a career and motherhood?"

She shrugged. "Women have been doing it for decades. I'm going to do most of my work from home because hey, I'm the boss, right?"

He stared deep into her eyes and loved the passionate glint reflected in them. "If anyone is capable of doing it, it's you."

Her face lit up from his vote of confidence, then just as quickly something else flickered across her face.

"What is it?" he asked.

Leila drew a breath and opened her mouth, but she said nothing and shook her head.

Garrick's curiosity inflamed. "Tell me."

Her dark gaze intensified as she studied him.

While she did so, Garrick witnessed a profound vulnerability wash over her. He brushed an errant lock of hair from her face. "What is it?"

"I don't regret my decision. I-It's just that I'm worried about…"

He waited while her eyes dropped to stare at nothing.

"All parents worry," he assured, lowering his hand to stroke her face. "I'm not a parent, but I get my information from pretty reliable sources."

Glancing up, Leila smiled, though her eyes shimmered with unshed tears.

Concern replaced Garrick's humor. "I'm sorry. I'm listening."

The top sheet drifted to lie lazily across their hips. "I worry about being like my mother," she confessed. She attentively watched his reaction and appreciated his patience while she gathered the strength to continue.

"My mother committed suicide when I was twelve—one year after my father was killed in a car crash."

Her words punched him hard in the gut and rendered him speechless.

"Sam found her and I found her letter—begging that we find it in our hearts to forgive her. Said something about how hard it was to look at us every day and see our father."

"She must have been devastated when he died," he finally said.

Leila's eyes hardened. "We all were. That didn't give her the right to bail on us. Our dad's death was an accident. She *chose* to leave us. How do you forgive that?"

He didn't recoil from her anger, but understood it. "I know it was hard."

"It *is* hard." She wiped at her tears. "Forgiving her is a daily act. For me as well as for Sam…which is why I don't understand—"

"How she could leave Emma?"

Leila nodded. "Roslyn is the middle child and seemingly more emotionally adjusted. Sam and I are extreme opposites. I try too hard…and she doesn't try at all."

"Try to what?"

"Not be like my mother." She found his gaze again. "I never want to harm a child like that, which is why I convinced myself that I didn't want to become a mom—then Emma showed up…."

Garrick smiled and leaned over to kiss her. "You don't have to worry. Your niece is very lucky to have you."

He kissed her again and could feel her body submit against him. This time when they came together there was an element of tenderness Garrick hadn't known that he was capable of feeling. She filled his senses and like a thief in the night stole what he wasn't prepared to give again: his heart.

Ciara arrived at Leila's shortly before ten o'clock with a stack of files from *Atlanta Spice*. She enjoyed working from Leila's home because it gave her the freedom to dress down. Today she wore a light blue baby-doll top that prominently displayed her growing belly.

As usual she gave a quick rap on the door and entered. Inside, she inhaled the fresh scent of roasted coffee beans. "Good morning," she sang, walking past the kitchen.

"Good morning," a deep baritone sang back.

Ciara froze and replayed the voice in her head. *Definitely not Leila.* She walked backward and stopped before the kitchen's doorway.

Mr. Fine from across the street smiled back at her. "Care for some coffee?"

She blinked and then her eyes roamed over him, dressed in a too-short, too-tight pink terry-cloth robe—twice. "No, thanks." She forced on a smile. "Where are Leila and Emma?"

"Upstairs." He poured two cups of coffee. "We all sort of slept late this morning. Are you sure you don't want any coffee?"

"I wish I could." She touched her stomach. "I'm expecting." His deepening dimples made him more devastatingly handsome.

"Congratulations!" He turned toward the refrigerator. "We have some orange juice, if you like."

We? Ciara's brows rose. "That would be great."

Upstairs, a door shut and footsteps rushed down the hall. "Garrick, you better get dressed. Ciara should be here soon," Leila called out.

Ciara glanced up and smiled at her boss. "Hello."

Leila blinked. "Oh, you're already here."

Ciara nodded. "Yep."

Emma began to babble enthusiastically.

"Hey, sweetie," Ciara cooed back.

Garrick strolled out of the kitchen and handed Ciara her orange juice before he glanced up at Leila. "Coffee?"

Leila's face flushed burgundy while her eyes shifted between her secretary and her new…what? She shook off the question and laughed. Whatever he was, she committed herself to loving every minute of it.

The next week, for Valentine's Day, Garrick pulled out all the stops by filling her house with her favorite flowers and taking her and Emma to the romantic Canoe restaurant off Atlanta's Chattahoochee River.

The lovemaking was especially sweet that night. Their bodies joined together in a tangled mass, where neither could tell where one began and the other ended.

For Leila, each coupling brought her to new orgasmic heights and gave her a peace she'd never known. And for Garrick, he discovered love was better the second time around.

Chapter 20

"It's so nice to finally meet you—again!" Tamara reached out and enclosed Leila and Emma into her embrace as they entered her home for dinner. "How long has it been—three months? I was beginning to think Garrick was ashamed of us or something."

"Not the way he keeps talking about you guys." Leila winked at Garrick from over his sister-in-law's shoulder. When she drew back, she took one look into Tamara's eyes and felt an immediate kinship.

"I know the last time we met was rather…"

"Interesting," Tamara finished for her. "And you must be little Emma." She pinched the baby's cheeks and was rewarded with a hearty belly laugh.

"She's adorable," Orlando commented, joining in on the cheek pinching. "You're going to have quite a time keeping the boys away from this one." He winked.

"She's already stolen my heart," Garrick said, and then paused. "Wait. Are we talking about Leila or Emma?"

Leila blushed while Tamara and Orlando laughed.

Omara joined the group and was tickled to death when Leila and Garrick allowed her to play with the baby. When dinner was ready, everyone moved into the dining room.

"You're now working full-time from your house?"

"As much as I can. There have been a few days when I had to take her into the office. Wackiness ensued, but we always seem to survive."

"So." Tamara stabbed her steak and pinned

Garrick with a simmering look. "Does this mean you've changed your mind about career women?"

Orlando's eyes widened as they shifted from his wife to Garrick.

"Yes, tell us." Leila carefully braided her hands above her plate. "Has dating me changed your mind about career women?" She smiled.

"Dating you has changed my mind about a lot of things." He winked. "Some I can't mention in front of mixed company."

Orlando chuckled. "Great backhand. One point for the bro-meister."

"Better get used to that," Tamara warned. "They love to keep score."

"Is that right?" Leila slid her foot beneath the table and then glided it up Garrick's leg. "I'd like to keep score myself some time."

"Two points for Leila."

Orlando looked up, stunned. "What?"

"She gets two points," Garrick repeated.

Leila placed on her sweetest smile.

Tamara's face lit with understanding and she raised her hand to receive a high five. "That's my girl!"

Orlando continued to be lost. "I don't understand. What just happened?"

The other adults collapsed with laughter. Throughout the rest of their meal, the Graysons made Leila feel right at home. The love radiating between Orlando and his wife put her in mind of Roslyn and Patrick, and even Ciara and Elmo.

At one point in the night, she couldn't remember why marriage had failed to be something she'd pursued. Once, Leila rarely thought about how life had been before her father's car accident, but she thought about it all the time now.

The truth was, once upon a time, Nicole and Reggie Owens were happy—deliriously so. Every day seemed filled with sunshine and laughter. Her father praised her every accomplishment and when there were tears, he was right there to kiss them away.

Leila, Roslyn, and Samantha—each were princesses and none of them could imagine a prince being as wonderful as their father.

Leila escaped her reverie to glance at Garrick across the table. He was a prince she hadn't prepared for. At that moment, Garrick caught her stare and winked. Even that harmless act caused a nest of butterflies to flutter madly in her stomach.

She loved this man—clueless of how and when it happened. She shook her head and then tried to pay attention to Tamara as she relayed the story of how she and Orlando met and fell in love.

However, Leila's own memories captured her attention again. She remembered her and her sisters sneaking out of bed to go watch her parents dance cheek to cheek in the living room. They always looked so happy and so in love.

Garrick leaned forward and took her hand. "Leila?"

"What?" She glanced around. "What did you say?"

He laughed. "You disappeared on me again."

"Sorry. It won't happen again."

It did. All night, Leila made constant comparisons between Garrick and her father, and surprisingly between herself and her mother. Yet, this time, she grew envious of her mom. Had her father loved her too much? Was there such a thing as too much?

"I loved your family," Leila admitted during

their ride home. "But how come your brother doesn't work with you at your father's firm?"

Garrick shrugged. "He never cared for the business. He's always been more of a sports jock and he loves teaching so he just combined the two and became a coach."

"You two are extremely close."

"He was my best friend."

"Was?"

"He's sort of been replaced by this beautiful woman that lives across the street from me. You might even know her."

Touched, she leaned across the seat, planted a kiss on his cheek, and confessed, "You're my best friend, too."

He smiled. "Do you think I can see my best friend naked tonight?"

"I'll show you mine, if you show me yours." She winked.

When they arrived at the house, Leila took her bundle of joy upstairs for her bath. This was quickly becoming another favorite time for Leila. Watching Emma sing and splash her hands in the water was a pure delight. As usual, Leila joined in on the action. When bath time was over, Leila was just as drenched as her niece.

Soon after, she laid Emma down for the night and went to join her man in the bedroom.

"How's our little girl doing?" Garrick asked, reclining back on the bed.

"Sleeping like an angel." She kicked off her shoes and peeled her dress straps off her shoulders.

"Come here. Let me help you with that." Effortlessly, he bounded off the bed, dressed only in a pair of black boxers.

Entranced, Leila moved toward him. Her heart thumped wildly inside her chest while her body tingled in apprehension. She pressed against his growing hardness, relishing the electric feel of his muscular arms as her hands ran up their length and then across his smooth, broad chest.

"Have I told you lately how beautiful you are?" Garrick whispered the question against her cheek. His long fingers fumbled with the back of her dress for a moment, but he was finally able to slide the small zipper down her backside.

He felt like a kid unwrapping his favorite toy. When the dress hit the floor, his hand seared a path around her waist and drew her closer. The scent of her completed the assault on his senses.

He wanted and needed to be buried deep inside of her, but he was willing to take his time to get there. His head descended and captured a sweet kiss.

Leila hooked her fingers into the band of his boxers and pushed them below his hips.

"We're a little eager this evening," Garrick laughed against her lips.

"I'm burning up," she whispered back.

"I think I can help you with that." He unsnapped her bra and let it join the dress on the floor. Gently, he cupped her full, lush breasts in his hands and fed one into his greedy mouth.

Leila's sigh filled the room and became the music of the night as Garrick's mouth danced between her breasts. Unable to endure the aching, Garrick laid her on the bed and shimmied her panties off her hips.

The triangle of curls nestled between her legs snapped Garrick's control. He loved the way her warm body sheathed him as he entered her. He moved; his hips rocked to the sound of their bodies' music. Stroke after luxurious stroke, he ground deeper in hopes of touching her very soul in the way she'd touched his own.

Spurred by desire and the crescendo of her cries, Garrick's thrust became a jackhammer. He gritted his teeth through the pain of Leila's nails digging into his back. She writhed uncontrollably and even tried to escape when her first orgasm surfaced. He quickly locked her hips into place and only had a short wait for her body's tremors to hurtle him into ecstasy, where he collapsed, temporarily spent.

The combination of the morning's warm sun rays and Emma's soft singing over the baby monitor penetrated the thick, lazy fog swirling inside Leila's mind.

Another glorious day—another blissful morning.

She knew without looking that Garrick wasn't in the room, but was either in the baby's room or making coffee in the kitchen.

Confirmation soon followed when Garrick's heavy baritone filtered through the monitor.

"Are you going to finish your bottle for your uncle Garrick? That's my girl."

Uncle Garrick? A warm glow radiated within her and she spread her arms out wide as if to embrace life. She could get used to this. She and Garrick and little Emma made a nice family.

Family?

She shook her head, amazed at how caught up she was in her flight of fancy. She'd even begun to wonder what it would be like if she spent more quality time with her niece. After all, her early formative years were important. Of course, the only way she could do that was if…she sold the company.

Leila let the thought linger in her head.

It was the first time the idea appealed to her. She could sell the company and negotiate a position for herself that wouldn't require a lot of her time.

The doorbell rang and Leila turned over to glance at the clock. It was Saturday, so Ciara shouldn't be downstairs.

The bell chimed again.

"Do you want me to get the door?" Garrick asked over the monitor.

How did he know I was up? "No. I'll get it," she shouted, and then forced herself out of bed. She quickly located her robe, raked her hands through her hair a few times and rushed out of the bedroom.

As she bolted past the baby's room, she blew a kiss.

"I'm going to take that as a rain check," he barked behind her.

"Deal!" She took the stairs two at a time as the bell rang a third time. "I'm coming," she bellowed, and then mumbled under her breath, "just hold your horses." At last, she jerked open the door and felt her smile melt from her face. "Samantha."

Chapter 21

"Hello, Leila." Samantha drew in a shaky breath and flittered a nervous smile. "How are you doing?"

"What are you doing here?" Leila's voice was hard and her stance defensive.

Her sister withered beneath her glare, but she didn't turn away. "I came to see…my daughter."

"Well, she doesn't want to see you." She slammed the door and stood behind it quaking with anger.

Sam knocked and rang the doorbell. "Let me

in, Leila. I'm not going anywhere until you do," she shouted through the door.

"Of course, you'll leave. That's what you're good at, remember?"

"Look, Leila. I know you're angry—"

"You think?" she screamed. "You dropped a baby off in my house with a lousy letter and disappeared for three months, and you think you can just waltz back here like nothing happened?"

Samantha didn't answer.

"What's going on?" Garrick asked, stepping into the foyer with a wide-eyed Emma in his arms.

Leila's stern expression collapsed at the beautiful image they posed and her heart squeezed at the thought of it being taken away.

Concern was written in the tiny lines around Garrick's eyes.

"Leila, please let me in," Samantha begged softly through the door.

"Who's at the door?" he asked.

Tears welled in Leila's eyes as she stared at them, but she couldn't make herself answer Garrick's question. When he headed toward her, she could do no more than shake her head.

"Let me see who's at the door," he said.

She thought about standing her ground; but when she realized that would only delay the inevitable, she moved aside.

Garrick opened the door.

Samantha blinked and straightened in surprise. "Oh, hello."

He slammed the door. "Is that who I think it is?"

Leila nodded. "It's Samantha."

"What is she doing here?"

"What do you think?"

They glanced at Emma, who gibbered as if she were holding an intelligent conversation.

"Guys, please let me in. I need to see Emma."

Garrick's and Leila's gazes landed on one another, their reluctance clearly written on their faces.

"We're going to have to let her in," he said.

"Says who?"

He cocked his head and narrowed his gaze.

"All right. Fine. Let her in." Leila crossed her arms and lifted her chin. "But she's not leaving here with Emma."

With a tight smile, Garrick opened the door.

Samantha jumped. When her gaze shifted to

her daughter, she gasped and cupped a hand across her mouth. "Oh, she's gotten so big."

"Oh, spare me the dramatics," Leila sneered. She walked over to Garrick and withdrew Emma from his arms. "You're not taking her." Leila spun and walked away.

"I'm her mother," Sam said, crossing the threshold.

"A fact you forgot three months ago," Garrick said.

Sam's head jerked toward him. "I'm sorry, but do I know you?"

"No. But your daughter does." He shut the door.

"Right." She injected steel into her backbone. "If you don't mind, this is a private conversation between me and my sister."

Fury glinted in his dark eyes and when he took a menacing step forward, Sam retreated. "But I do mind, Sam. I've come to care a great deal about what happens to your daughter and what you put your sister through."

She drew an angry breath, yet she clamped her mouth shut and stormed after her sister. "Do you mind getting your guard dog off my butt so *we* can talk?" she asked Leila when she exploded into the living room.

Leila warred with the request while she still clutched Emma in her arms.

"No need." Garrick tossed up his hands. "I was just about to go jump in the shower anyway." He backed up as his hard gaze stabbed Sam. "It's been a pleasure meeting you."

Leila rolled her eyes and patiently waited until she heard the bedroom door click closed upstairs. "You have some nerve showing up like this."

"I miss my daughter."

"I could care less," she snapped. Her body vibrated with rage. Confused, Emma twisted her face and began to cry. "Shh, sweetheart. It's okay."

Sam stepped forward with her arms outstretched. "Let me—"

"When hell freezes over."

"She can sense you're upset," Sam admonished as she moved forward. "Right, wrong or indifferent, she's still *my* daughter. Let me see her." Again, she held out her arms.

When Emma leaned forward to go to her, Leila winced from the sting of betrayal.

"Aw. You missed your mommy, too?" Sam cooed at her daughter.

Leila composed herself despite the fact her vision blurred with tears. "Why are you doing this? Why did you…?"

"Why did I have to come back?" Sam finished the question for her. "Isn't the answer obvious? I made a mistake."

"You mean you made *another* mistake." Leila turned and marched over to the fireplace. She extracted Sam's letter from the top of the mantel and turned back toward her. "Shall I read from the good book of Sam about the last mistake?"

"That's not necessary."

"Why, sure it is, since you like to change your mind about motherhood just as often as I had to change Emma's diaper." She unfolded the letter and read in her best dramatic voice. "Dear Leila, I'm sorry." She peered over the thin piece of paper. "No argument here so far."

"Leila—"

"Like me, motherhood was never a part of your plans. However, unlike me, your decision wasn't based on the fact that you would make a lousy mother, but simply because you're married to your career." Leila held up a finger. "Here comes my favorite part—I, on the other hand, am a *screwup*. I always have been."

"All right, you made your point," Sam shouted.

Once again, Emma started to cry.

Before Leila or Sam could react, a door slammed and the rush of heavy footsteps echoed through the house. Next thing they knew, Garrick was across the hallway, down the steps and in the living room.

"I'll take her," he said, pulling Emma into his arms with a look that dared Sam to object.

Emma instantly quieted as she rode back up the stairs in her uncle Garrick's arms. When the door slammed again, Samantha looked to her older sister. "Who *is* that guy?"

"A...friend."

Sam's eyebrows rose with disbelief. "Just a friend, huh?"

Leila crumpled the letter in her hand. "Don't turn this around. I don't have to explain myself—you do. You have another thing coming if you think you can waltz in here and I'm just going to hand Emma over to you."

Sam's demeanor cooled. "We can always call

the police and see what they'll say. I'll bet you they'll give me my daughter."

Calmly, Leila walked up to her sister, stared her down and, without thinking, whipped her open palm hard across Sam's face.

Sam's head snapped back and her eyes instantly glossed with tears as she placed a hand over her cheek.

Leila gasped when she realized what she'd done.

"Do you feel better now?" Sam croaked.

Leila dropped her gaze to stare at her hand. What was she doing? Why did she let Sam get the best of her? She choked on a sob as she sat down on the sofa. "I shouldn't have hit you."

Her sister hovered above her in silence, and then sank onto the cushion next to her. "That's all right. I deserved it—and much more."

"Does that mean I can hit you again?"

Sam looked up to see if she was serious and inched away in precaution.

"I was joking," Leila said without a hint of amusement.

"Sure you were." She scooted away some more. "That's quite an arm you have there."

Leila smiled, but then caught herself. "Don't get all charming on me now," she said seriously. "What you did…was unforgivable. What you're doing—?"

"I know. I know. But…I truly thought that I was doing the right thing when I brought Emma here. C'mon, you know I've never stayed in one place long, I can't hold down a job, and I always fall for the wrong men."

"Who's her father?"

Suddenly, Sam found her toes fascinating. "His name is Emmanuel James."

"Does he know about Emma?"

Samantha didn't answer.

Leila rolled her eyes and wondered why she'd asked.

"I know I should have told you and Roslyn about Emma, but I just didn't want to sit through another speech about how much of a screwup I am."

"So dropping her off in my kitchen was a better idea?"

"I wasn't thinking."

"That's my point." Leila jumped to her feet and paced again. "You never think things through. And how could you do it—especially what we went through after Mom—"

"I know. I know."

"Apparently not! Did you forget how many nights you cried when she abandoned us? How many times did you ask me whether it was your fault? Fast forward and you chose to do the same thing to your daughter? What did you expect for me to tell her when she got older? What did you want me to say when she asked whether it was her fault?"

Tears raced down her sister's plump cheeks.

"You're back now—but for how long? Six months from now will you think that you made another mistake?"

"No." Sam firmly shook her head.

"How can you be so sure?" Her words turned bitter on her tongue. "You're no better than she was. You're just like Momma—selfish to the end."

"No. I'm not like her," Sam said, standing. "I came back."

Chapter 22

Leila watched Sam and Emma from her bedroom window as they pulled out of her driveway. The experience felt as if someone were taking an ice pick to her heart and chipping it out one piece at a time. She sucked in a brave breath, but her chin trembled uncontrollably.

I should have seen this coming. I should have been better prepared.

"It's going to be all right."

Garrick looped a protective arm around her shoulders and she quickly shrugged it off. "I think you better go now." She turned away and raced to the bathroom. At the toilet, she dropped to her knees and threw up.

Garrick was a mere second behind her. "Are you all right?"

She shook her head and spewed out the last remnants of Tamara's meatloaf. Her stomach cramped, her head ached and a river of tears gushed down her eyes. How could she not know how badly she wanted something until it was taken away?

Through her sobs, she heard water running in the sink. Soon after, a cool towel was placed against her face.

"It's all right," Garrick assured, wiping her face. "You'll see. Everything will be all right."

"How do you know?" Leila's voice croaked and she took the towel from him to finish doing the job herself.

"Because I know you've gotten through worse things." He fought not to be hurt by her accusatory eyes or her hard tone. "Emma is still your niece. You'll see her again."

A pathetic laugh escaped her as she shook her head at his ignorance concerning Sam. "Maybe—maybe not." She tried to stand up. When he offered his arm to assist, she didn't take it.

Garrick struggled to understand what was happening and was having a devil of a time hanging on to his patience. Leila maneuvered around him to the sink, taking great care to avoid contact.

"You mind telling me what's going on?" he asked, crossing his arms.

She grabbed her toothbrush and her tube of toothpaste. "What does it look like?"

"Honestly? It looks like you're going through great extremes to piss me off." He folded his arms when she didn't respond but turned on the water.

He closed his eyes and drew a deep breath. However, he failed to calm down, so he tried it again. "Talk to me," he said softly, and then looked over at her again.

Leila scrubbed her teeth as if she held a vicious vendetta against them. "There's nothing to talk about," she garbled around the toothbrush.

"I'm trying to be here for you, but you're treating me like I had something to do with this."

She spat into the sink and reached for the mouthwash.

"Aren't you going to say something?"

She turned up a Dixie cup of mouthwash and swished it around.

"I don't have time for this. You can call me when you're ready to talk." He stomped out of the bathroom and combed the bedroom for his shoes.

Leila stormed right behind him, jerked open her drawers, and began hurling his clothes at him.

"What the—?"

"There's no reason for you to keep leaving your stuff here. You just live across the street."

A pair of jeans smacked him against the head. "What the hell is wrong with you?"

"Why does it have to be something wrong with me? I'm simply saying you have a perfectly good house across the street with a perfectly good bedroom with a perfectly functional chest of drawers," she said, ending in almost hysteria.

He froze, not sure how he should proceed, but fully realized he stood in a dangerous minefield. "Leila, I know you're upset with Samantha—"

"I'm not upset!" She threw clothes at him—the majority of them belonged to her.

"Let's sit down so we can talk about it?"

She pivoted and stared at him as though he'd grown a second head. "If I'm not upset, why do I need to talk?"

Because you're losing your marbles.

"Look," she attempted in a more patient tone, "I just want you to keep *your* things at *your* place—in fact why don't you stay there from now on?"

Stunned, he stared at her. "You're breaking up with me?"

"Well." She shifted her weight, crossed, and recrossed her arms. "There's no real reason for us to keep playing house anymore."

"I wasn't—"

"Oh, come off of it." She paced. "You liked it over here because it was a nice ready-made family so you could live out your dreams of being a father—or an *uncle*."

"That's b.s. and you know it!"

"Oh, please." She stopped pacing and returned to throwing everything out of her drawers.

"I like it over here because apparently I'm attracted to *crazy* women."

"Oh, now I'm crazy?"

"Are you kidding me? Is this a real argument? You have to be the most neurotic woman I've ever met."

"It's over, Garrick. The last three months was nothing but a lie. I allowed myself to get caught up in some stupid fantasy when I should have known better. In the end everyone leaves me. My father, my mother, and my sisters."

"I don't understand—your sisters?"

She stopped what she was doing and leaned against her vanity table. "After… It was just the three of us for a long time. The state didn't break us up. We managed to bounce to and fro in the same foster homes. When I turned eighteen, I got my own place. My sisters were allowed to live with me. It didn't last long. Roslyn married Patrick before she even graduated from high school—and Samantha hightailed it a year later. And as you know, she never stays in one place long." She finally faced him again. "The only thing that's been constant in my life has been my magazine." She shook her head and mumbled to herself. "And here I was thinking about giving that up."

"What?"

"Nothing."

Leila raked her hands through her hair—it sort of reminded him of the first time he'd met her. He stepped forward, but she stopped him with a look.

"Emma's gone," she said. "And now it's time for me to get back to my life."

"I would never stop you from living your life."

"Not intentionally. But why waste your time? We want different things. You want a family and I don't."

"That's not true." He gazed into her troubled brown eyes and saw the vulnerable child within. "I saw how you lit up with Emma. I've witnessed the transformation in you and how you took care of her."

"And where did that leave me? Standing here in my bedroom, feeling like I did when I read my mother's suicide letter."

Garrick's tears stung the backs of his eyes. "If you're looking at me for some type of guarantee, I can't—"

"That's right. You can't." Leila drew a deep breath and suddenly had a hard time meeting his eyes. "If I thought that we—that you could handle a no-strings-attached kind of relationship or that you could accept being runner-up to my job—"

"Leila, don't do this." He braced himself for heartbreak, but had no clue on how to go about doing that. "You're upset and you're saying things that you don't mean."

"I want a clean break," she said and nearly choked on a sob. "I want my old life back. The one before Emma or *you* came along."

Garrick clenched his teeth as he glared at her. "Your wish is my command." He turned.

"Wait," she called after him.

Against his will, a small bubble of hope rose.

"Don't forget your stuff," she added softly.

The callous way she dismissed him—and what had transpired between them—hardened something within him. He turned back and glanced at everything thrown across the room before he looked at her. "Keep it. I don't want anything that reminds me of you."

Chapter 23

"You don't think you might be overreacting?" Orlando asked, grabbing a beer out of the fridge. "I mean, you just moved here."

"The place is too big for one person," Garrick lied, knowing his brother wouldn't buy it. "I purchased a condominium in Buckhead that cuts my drive time to the office in half. Plus, I'll be closer to you and Tamara."

"Oh, joy. That means you'll be over for dinner twice as much."

"Don't worry. I'll bring the wine."

"Uh-huh." Orlando crossed his arms. "You know it's hard enough for me to get some alone time with my wife when there's a three-year-old constantly wanting to sleep with us."

Garrick chuckled. "I hardly think my coming over is actually going to cramp your scheduled five minutes of hot burning love."

"Ten minutes. And it's not the quantity so much as the quality."

"Like your Tarzan and Jane nights?" Garrick winked and also grabbed a beer out of the icebox. "Trust me. I'm not interested in interrupting those precious moments."

"Glad to hear it." Orlando moseyed around the breakfast bar and drew several deep breaths while he stared at his brother.

"What is it?" Garrick asked, though he had an idea of what was coming.

"What is what?"

"Oh, we're going to play that game now?"

Orlando dropped his shoulders during one long exhalation. "When are you going to tell me what happened between you and Leila?"

Though Garrick knew the question was coming, it still felt like a blow to the gut just at the mere mention of her name. "There's nothing to tell." He turned up his bottle for a long swig.

"So we're switching to that game now?" Orlando met and held Garrick's gaze. "Things looked pretty hot and heavy between you two. What happened?"

In the past two weeks, Garrick had posed that question to himself numerous times and he was no closer to answering it than when he'd stormed out of Leila's house. "It was a mistake—*we* were a mistake."

"Really?" Orlando's gaze remained heavy as he combed his brother's face, looking and finding cracks in his mask of indifference. "I liked her. Tamara did, too."

What was he supposed to say to that? Garrick lowered his head, suddenly fascinated with the kitchen's floor tile.

"Have you tried to talk with her?"

He drew a deep breath, but didn't respond.

"Love isn't always sunshine. It takes work and commitment—and letting her believe that she's always right."

A weak smile wobbled across Garrick's lips. "It's not that simple."

"Of course it's not, but you should at least go down swinging. Anything worth having is worth fighting for."

"C'mon." Garrick set down his bottle on the countertop. "We only knew each other for a few months—and one of those, we weren't even talking."

"But it was long enough for you to fall in love."

"Who said anything about…?"

Orlando shot him a look that said, *Don't even try it.*

Garrick grabbed his beer again and drained the contents in one long gulp, while he replayed the blowup between him and Leila in his mind. "Too much was said," he concluded.

"It always is."

He glanced up, shaking his head. "What are you, Dr. Phil now?"

"I'm not going to lie, we TiVo the show every afternoon."

Garrick frowned.

"What can I say? Marriage is also about compromises and it's cheaper than counseling. Besides, it's not so bad once you get into it."

Orlando hopped onto a bar stool. "So what do you say? You're going to call her up—or walk across the street?"

Garrick considered the question, but then slowly shook his head. "She wants me to play second fiddle to her career. I can't do that—not again."

The doorbell rang.

Garrick smiled. "That should be the Realtor." He walked past his brother, pretending not to see him shake his head or hear him mumble under his breath.

"You're making a big mistake."

"It looks like we have ourselves a deal." Mr. Porter stood from his chair and jutted his hand across Leila's desk. "You sure know how to drive a hard bargain."

Her smile uneven, Leila stood and accepted his hand. "I admire your persistence."

"All in a day's work." He winked and then grabbed his briefcase. "I'm heading out to New York tonight. The contracts should be here by the end of the week."

Leila nodded, walked around her desk and

then escorted him to the door. "I have to tell you that it's been great doing business with you." She opened the door.

"Likewise."

The moment he exited, Leila closed the door and felt sick. Guilt and doubt churned inside her at such a dizzying rate, she rushed to the other side of her office and bolted inside her private bathroom.

Once she'd finished dumping her lunch, Ciara's excited voice echoed off the bathroom's acoustics. "You did it, didn't you?"

Leila moaned and rested her head against the cold porcelain. "Did you come in here to lecture me?"

"Are you kidding me? Ninety-seven million dollars and you're still the editor-in-chief—what's there to lecture about?"

"Co-editor-in-chief. I'm going to take on a lighter schedule." Leila climbed to her feet and quickly cleaned herself up.

Ciara blinked in astonishment. "The Energizer Bunny wants a lighter schedule? What gives?"

"Nothing." Leila shrugged and maneuvered

around Ciara's bulging belly to exit the small bathroom. "Besides, weren't you the one who said I needed to slow down?"

"Yeah, but since when do you listen to me?"

"Since now." Leila plopped into her chair. "I need a staff meeting scheduled for tomorrow, buzz Deonté and tell him I'm still waiting for the photo layouts for the Cavalli Spring collection, and tell Jeannie if her feature isn't in my office by five, I'll personally break both of her legs."

"Maybe I should ask you what's your definition of a light schedule."

"Until the acquisition is finalized, it's still business as usual," Leila answered briskly and then drew a deep breath to calm her nerves.

Ciara studied her. "Are you all right? You look like crap."

"I'm fine," she snapped, and then placed her phone off Do Not Disturb.

Ciara walked to the desk and put it back on.

"What the hell are you doing? I have work to do."

"Not until you tell me what's really going on with you. And need I remind you, I can stand here all day."

* * *

After two weeks of her sister dodging her calls, Roslyn paid a visit to *Atlanta Spice,* determined to get some answers. Well aware Leila could be difficult, Roslyn was prepared to camp out in her sister's office all day if the situation warranted it.

Patrick had warned her to prepare for Samantha's reappearance—especially if she became too attached to Emma, but it never occurred to Roslyn to prepare Leila. It should have, but it didn't.

Leila, for all her proclamations of being Ms. Independent and her adamant stance on not wanting children. Roslyn wondered why she didn't recognize it as b.s. sooner.

Ciara wasn't at her desk, so Roslyn took it upon herself to knock once and enter her sister's office. "Great, you're here."

Ciara smiled. "Looks like I have reinforcements."

Leila groaned.

Frowning, Roslyn closed the door. "Reinforcements for what?" She glanced questioningly at her sister and was surprised by what she saw. "Good Lord, you look like crap."

"It's good to see you, too," Leila smirked, and then changed the subject. "What are you doing here?"

"Now that Patrick is back home, I came to see why you haven't returned any of my calls."

"I've been busy." Leila fiddled with her pen and avoided eye contact. "How is his father?"

"On the road to recovery."

"Have you heard from Samantha?"

Roslyn's heart squeezed at the hurt and pain reflected in her sister's voice, and wished she could somehow fix it.

Leila looked up.

"No, I haven't," Roslyn answered, and then tried to inject hope in her next words. "You know Sam. She'll turn up again."

Leila's eyes glossed over as she tilted up her chin. "Whatever. I have work to do." She wasn't going to let the situation get the best of her. She was a survivor and had been through worse.

"Tell you what," Roslyn said, staying committed to cheering her up. "Why don't you and Garrick come over tonight for dinner? The girls…what's the matter?"

The remnants of Leila's cool facade

crumbled and a waterfall of tears poured down her face. "Nothing's the matter." She snatched a Kleenex from its box on the desk. "I'm fine."

"You don't look fine."

Ciara rushed around the desk and threw a comforting arm around her boss. "She and Garrick broke up a couple of weeks ago."

"What?" Roslyn joined them around the desk, feeling very much the outsider. "Why didn't you tell me?"

"It's not a big deal," she lied, snatching more tissues and choking on her sobs. "We were completely wrong for each other."

Roslyn glanced over at Ciara and the secretary only shrugged.

"That's about as much as I've been able to get out of her, too."

Leila was aware that she was making quite a fool out of herself, but damn if she could stop. "He wants someone who will stay home, bear babies, and cater to his every need. That's not me."

"Did he say that?"

"Yeah."

Ciara and Roslyn looked dubiously at her.

"Well, not exactly. But it was something along those lines." She sniffed and could feel her body turn jittery. "Doesn't matter. I told him if he couldn't accept being runner-up to my job—"

"You said that?" Ciara and Roslyn shouted.

Leila winced. "It's the truth. My work is everything to me."

"Then why did you just sell the company?" Ciara asked.

"You what?"

Leila's stomach lurched and she jumped up from her chair and raced into the bathroom.

More confused than ever, Roslyn glanced at Ciara; but the secretary's eyes widened to the size of silver dollars.

"Oh-my-God!" Ciara stood and rushed behind Leila. She found her, once again, hovered above the toilet.

Roslyn quickly brought up the rear and it took her no time at all to leapfrog to the same conclusion. "Leila, are you pregnant?"

Chapter 24

"Don't be ridiculous!" Leila climbed to her feet, splashed cold water on her face, and swished some Listerine. When she was done, she stared at her reflection in the mirror. "You guys are right. I do look like crap."

When she turned, Ciara and Roslyn stood blocking the only exit.

"Do you two mind?"

"Have you even taken a test?"

"What test?"

In sync, Roslyn and Ciara cocked their heads and crossed their arms.

"There's no need for a pregnancy test. I'm not pregnant." No sooner had the words left her mouth, Leila's stomach lurched again, and she made another dive for the toilet bowl.

Roslyn turned to Ciara. "Do you mind—?"

"I'm already on my way."

"Wait. Where are you going?" Leila croaked while unable to get off her knees.

"She's going to the drugstore for a pregnancy test." Roslyn opened a few cabinets and located the towels. She made a cold compress and then joined her sister on the floor. "When was your last period?"

"What are you a doctor now?"

Roslyn placed her hand beneath her sister's chin and forced her to make eye contact. "Answer the question."

Leila jerked her head from Roslyn's grasp. "Don't baby me. I'm the oldest, remember?"

"Then how come you're acting like Samantha?"

Leila stiffened and finally met her sister's gaze. In an instant, she felt stripped and vulnerable. How long and how hard had she worked not to feel like this?

"Ros, I screwed up." Once again her eyes filled with tears. "I pushed him away. I don't know why I did it, but I did and now he'll never come back."

Roslyn gathered her sister into her arms. "Shh. It's going to be all right."

"No, it's not," Leila cried, clutching Roslyn as if she were a life raft. "I couldn't stop myself. I just felt like sooner or later he was going to leave me and I wanted to get it over with. I can't be pregnant. I can't."

"Shh. Don't worry about it. Everything is going to work out." She eased Leila back. "It always does, doesn't it?"

Through her sobs, Leila thought the question over and grudgingly admitted her sister had a point.

"Let me ask you—do you love him?"

She nodded with her face twisted in anguish. "So much it hurts."

"Then you just need to tell him."

Leila pulled away and shook her head. "You didn't hear what I said to him. He hates me."

"Honey, I saw how you two bicker. If anything I'd say you two were in a stalemate. Both of you are waiting for the other one to apologize."

"Is that why he put his place up for sale?"

Roslyn blinked. "Oh. He's good."

"W-What?"

"Nothing. Why don't you tell me exactly what happened between you two?"

Garrick was well aware of how his staff tiptoed around him, including Ned. He did, however, take great pleasure in ripping Arquette a new one when he yet again questioned the measurements on the Reynolds project.

For the most part, Garrick was content to bury himself in work, sleep four hours, and start the whole thing over again. This was what he should have been doing rather than trying to jump back into the dating arena. Some lessons were hard learned.

The phone rang and he snatched it up on the first ring.

"Make it fast. I'm under a tight deadline," he said.

"Mr. Grayson? This is Jessica at Emerson Realty. I wanted to let you know that we have a bid on the house."

His chest pinched at the news. "That was fast."

"It's a great house in a great neighborhood. They're willing to pay the asking price. We should know within three days if they have their financing."

He held the phone, not sure of how to respond.

"Mr. Grayson? Isn't this great news?"

"Yeah. Great."

An awkward silence hung over the line.

"Well, okay. I guess I'll give you a call in three days."

Garrick nodded and hung up the phone. For a while, all he could do was stare at it and feel as if he'd just been told he'd lost a loved one. "You're doing the right thing," he reaffirmed.

Yet his heart wasn't so sure.

He leaned back and stretched out his long limbs. *Three days.* He sighed. Suddenly, everything seemed so final. He didn't fight the memories of Leila this time. He let them all flood his senses. From the minute he'd met her outside her house screaming like a madwoman, to the moment she'd kicked him out of her house—almost screaming like a madwoman.

He laughed and then wondered if something was wrong with him.

Truth was Leila Owens was a mixed bag of contradictions. He'd never met a woman who could push you away while her eyes begged for you to stay. She claimed she was a die-hard career woman with no aspirations of being a mother—but one look at her holding her niece and anyone would know that she was lying.

How long would you have to lie to yourself before you believed it to be true?

So why had he left if he knew that she really didn't want him to?

A light tap on the door saved him from pondering the question any further.

Ned poked his head through the door. "I'm getting ready to head out. You staying?"

"Yeah. Yeah." Garrick shuffled some papers around on his desk. "I still have quite a bit to do."

His buddy nodded and continued to linger at the door.

"Is there something else?" Garrick asked.

"Well, now that you mention it." Ned pushed open the door and entered. "Want to tell me what's up with you?"

Great. Another person who wants to psycho-analyze me.

"Everything is fine, Ned. I just want to catch up on some work."

"So how's Leila doing?" he asked as if he hadn't heard Garrick.

"Leila and I broke up," he admitted. "And before you get started...I'm cool with it."

"Yeah. That was very convincing." Ned eased into a chair across from his desk. "Since I'm a man of very few words, I'll get right to the point. Do you love her?"

"I... That has nothing to do with it."

"Are you kidding me?" Ned laughed. "Did you learn nothing from your first marriage? Love has everything to do with it."

Tears burned Leila's eyes as she stared at the blue stripe on the home pregnancy test. Problem was she was uncertain whether they were tears of joy or despair. She was forty years old and pregnant. It actually sounded like a punch line.

She jumped at the knock on the bathroom door, and then relaxed when she remembered Roslyn and Ciara waited on the other side.

"Leila, are you all right?" Roslyn asked softly.

"Y-Yes. I'm fine." Leila sucked in a deep breath, fixed her face and opened the door.

Two sets of curious and expectant eyes landed and followed Leila as she exited the bathroom and made her way to her desk.

Roslyn and Ciara glanced at each other and then back at Leila.

"Well?" Roslyn asked.

Leila looked down at the test she still clutched in her hand as if to double-check the results. "Positive."

Roslyn and Ciara squealed, clutched each other, and jumped for joy.

"Hello. Remember me?" Leila asked, agitated to be left out of the celebration.

"Of course, we remember you." A misty-eyed Roslyn flew around the desk to clench her sister into a fierce embrace that nearly cut off her air supply. Roslyn released her before she passed out, but she was quickly snatched into Ciara's arms.

"I can't believe we're both pregnant. You simply have to see my obstetrician. You'll love her."

"Yes. And it's never too early to look for a pediatrician," Roslyn informed her.

"Let's not forget the schools. All the good ones have a waiting list. Get your name on them now and you should be in like Flynn."

"Whoa. Whoa. Slow it down." Leila pushed herself out of her chair and raked her hands through her hair. "You guys are going too fast for me. I have other things to handle before figuring out doctors and schools."

The women settled down at her grave expression.

"I mean, how am I going to break this news to Garrick?"

Roslyn sat back on her haunches. "He's not going to be happy?"

"Are you kidding me?" Leila laughed. "He's going to be ecstatic."

Again Roslyn and Ciara glanced at each other.

"So…what's the problem?" Ciara asked cautiously.

"The problem is that I don't want him to use this as an excuse for us to get back together."

"So now you want to get back with him?" Roslyn asked, trying to keep up.

"Of course I wanted us to get back together— I just didn't know how to go about doing it."

"Has anyone ever told you that you're neurotic?" Ciara asked.

Roslyn touched Ciara's shoulder and nodded. "Plenty of times."

"Ha. Ha. Make jokes." Leila stopped pacing and thought about the small life starting inside of her. Her smile was instant and an undeniable warmth radiated through her. She was going to be a mother.

"I think I need to sit down again."

The women helped her to a chair.

"So when do you think you're going to tell him?" Ciara asked after an awkward silence had passed.

"I don't know," Leila said dully.

"*Are* you going to tell him?" Roslyn asked.

Leila shrugged as those damn tears came back again. "I don't know."

The room fell silent again until, at last, there was a knock on the door.

"Tell whoever it is I'm busy," Leila groaned as she buried her face into the palms of her hands.

"Will do." Ciara rushed to the door; however, she was shocked into silence the moment she opened it.

"Hey, is Leila in?"

Roslyn's head jerked to the door. "Who is it?"

At her sister's sharp gasp, Leila glanced up. "Samantha."

Chapter 25

Samantha stood frozen at the door as if attacked by a sudden case of stage fright. The air in the room thickened with tension and became difficult for them all to breathe. Emma, oblivious to what was going on, squirmed with excitement in her mother's arms.

"Hey!" Emma shouted and gave Leila a wide two-teeth grin.

Leila's heart squeezed as she smiled lovingly back at her.

"I didn't know both of you would be here," Sam croaked nervously.

Roslyn crossed her arms. "Sorry to have disappointed you," she said, unable to deflect the hurt in her tone.

"I'll leave you guys alone," Ciara announced. "Call me tonight if you need anything—books, referrals, or even bail money." She flashed Samantha a meaningful look and then eased around her.

Leila watched until the door closed before she lit into her sister. "What is it now, Sam? You came to drop Emma off again, or do you need money?"

"Maybe you're in trouble with the law or you need a place to stay?" Roslyn jumped in on the act.

"No, it's nothing like that." Sam closed her eyes as hurt rippled across her face.

Leila, despite her nausea, toughened her resolve. There was no way she was going to let her sister manipulate and use her again. She had her own set of problems. "Then what is it?"

Sam fidgeted some more and hedged for a while before she shook her head and turned back toward the door. "Sorry. This was a mistake."

"That's right. Run away." Leila tossed up her arms. "That's what you're good at." The moment the words were out of her mouth, she felt like a hypocrite. Wasn't that what she'd done with Garrick?

Sam didn't face them again, but Emma played hide-and-seek over her mother's shoulder.

The little game made it difficult for Leila to hold on to her anger.

"I'm tired of running," Sam whispered to the door. "I don't know why I do it. All I know is that I can't keep doing it."

Leila caught something that she'd never heard in Samantha's voice. Was it sincerity? She shook her head, not believing that she was actually falling for this.

"So what are you going to do?" Roslyn asked, her voice tight.

"I've stopped."

Slowly, Sam turned around and met Leila's gaze dead-on. In that moment, Leila knew her baby sister had grown up. "What brought all of this on?" she asked, standing from her chair.

"I had a little help." Sam's face lit up like a

ray of sunshine as she glanced lovingly at her daughter.

Leila's resolve finally softened when she reflected on just how much Emma had changed her life as well.

"Emma…and her father have really helped me see how much my past was ruling and destroying my future."

"Her father?" Leila and Roslyn asked in equally shocked voices.

Samantha tinted as she lifted her right hand and showed off a diamond ring.

"You're married!" the sisters shouted in unison and then flew to her with outstretched arms.

"Who's married?" Ciara ducked back into the room—a dead giveaway that she had been listening outside the door—and joined in the celebration hugs.

Emma giggled as if the human stockpile was a new game.

"You have to tell us everything," Roslyn declared, leading Sam to the plush leather couch.

Leila took Emma from Sam's arms and showered her with kisses before settling on the cushion next to Sam.

"I can't wait for you two to meet Emmanuel," Sam said, glowing. "He is the most loving, patient, and kind man I have ever met. We met in Chicago. I thought we were just having some fun, you know. He'd just gone through a divorce and wasn't looking for anything serious and you know I'm never looking for anything serious. Then I got pregnant—freaked, and ran to Las Vegas." She lowered her head. "It was weird. The entire time I was pregnant I was convinced that I could take care of my baby and that I wasn't going to make the same mistakes Mom made—just so many plans. But that isn't what happened at all."

Sam extracted her daughter from Leila and held her close. "After she was born—I felt this awful disconnect, a deep indescribable level of depression. It was so all-consuming. I couldn't think straight."

"Postpartum depression," Ciara said, nodding. "I've heard some horror stories."

"Initially I thought it would fade with time, but it didn't." Sam met Leila's gaze again. "I left Emma with you because I feared what I might do. To her as well as to myself. Leaving her was one of the saddest days of my life."

"Why didn't you tell me all of this a couple of weeks ago?"

"You and your boyfriend had already tried and sentenced me before I walked in the door," she said with a laugh. "I see why you like him though. On top of being extremely handsome, he's very protective of you. He must love you very much."

Leila grew warm at the unexpected observation and battled not to become a babbling idiot for the umpteenth time that day. Garrick Grayson did love her. She had instinctively known that from the first time they'd made love. What was worse: she had fallen in love with him as well.

"So when did you get married?" Roslyn asked.

"Well, in the three months I was gone. I did some heavy soul-searching. I even went back to the house where Mom…"

Roslyn and Leila glanced at each other and then reached for Sam's hand; both were riveted by her next words.

"The house is empty."

"And on the bad side of town," Roslyn reminded her.

"Yeah. But the minute I walked into that place…I felt her presence. I just started crying, weeping, and wailing until I didn't have anything left." Tears splashed down Samantha's face. "After that…an unbelievable peace settled over me. That's when I came back for Emma and then took her up to Chicago for the first time to meet her father." She smiled and wiped her face. "As it turns out, he'd combed the whole city looking for me."

"Oh, I think I'm going to cry." Ciara jumped up and rushed for the Kleenex box from Leila's desk. "This has been a day of great news. First, Leila's pregnancy and now this."

Samantha's eyes snapped wide in shock. "What?"

Leila shrank with embarrassment, shrugged, and then managed to squeak out, "Surprise."

Whatever work Garrick had planned to finish was long forgotten by the time Ned left his office. Now he was consumed with memories of his short, whirlwind romance with his hot, complicated neighbor. On one hand, the woman was completely wrong for him; but on the other, she was his soul mate.

Giving up for the night, Garrick grabbed his things and locked up. The idea of dinner with Orlando and his family while they, too, continued on the "Leila was the best thing that ever happened to you" campaign didn't sit well either.

The moment Garrick slid behind the wheel of his car, he decided a long drive was the type of therapy he needed. In no time, Leila rode to the forefront of his mind. The woman had actually run a criminal report on him and, of course, her laugh. Those deep musical tones had a way of bringing an instant smile to his face.

And then there was the lovemaking.

By day, Leila Owens was a dominant woman, but by night she was submissive in all the ways he found pleasing. Even now, alone in his car, he longed to hear his name whispered from her lips during the throes of passion.

Garrick lost count of how many times he drove around the Atlanta perimeter, but suddenly everything clicked in his mind and he knew what he had to do. He was just sorry that it had taken him so long to figure it out.

* * *

Leila liked Emmanuel. More importantly, she believed wholeheartedly that he truly loved Sam. Patrick was perhaps the hardest on the man. He spent the whole evening drilling Emmanuel about what he did for a living, how much money he made, and what plans he had in place for Sam and Emma.

The proceedings were adorable and Emmanuel was a doll for putting up with it. Leila was extremely happy for her sister and perhaps a little envious.

She cut out on the dinner celebration at Roslyn's a little early. She felt guilty for blaming her sudden fatigue on her "condition," but she needed some alone time to think.

"Leila," Roslyn called and rushed out to the car. "Are you all right?" she asked when she reached her. "I mean, you seem a little distant tonight."

"Have a lot on my mind," Leila answered honestly.

Roslyn nodded, but seemed to hesitate to say more.

"What is it?" Leila prompted.

"Well, you never said whether you were happy about the pregnancy."

Leila chuckled and then slung an arm around her sister. "I'm thrilled about becoming a mother. It's my next frontier, right?"

"And I'm going to be right there beside you."

"So am I." Sam's voice floated over to them. She moved from behind Roslyn to slip her arm around Leila as well.

"I love you two," Leila said and kissed them good-night. She didn't immediately go home. Instead, she thought a long drive was just the therapy she needed. In no time, Garrick rode to the forefront of her mind. Strangely, she wondered if he'd ever taken care of the one traffic ticket he had outstanding.

She chuckled and then languished in a few memories that made her laugh, smile, and tingle. Then, like always, she replayed the last memory of them together and she winced at some of the words that had spilled out of her mouth.

"Maybe it's true—I am neurotic."

She lost count of how many times she drove around Atlanta's perimeter, but suddenly everything clicked in her mind and she knew what she had to do. She was just sorry that it had taken her so long to figure it out.

Leila sucked in a deep breath as she walked up the short stone steps of her old childhood home. The white brick house looked smaller than she remembered, the neighborhood rougher.

"I can do this," she whispered and reached for the doorknob. It turned and opened with a loud squeak.

She glanced around the dark neighborhood and the even darker house. It had been a nice house once—great structure.

Leila moved slowly about the room. In her head, she changed the dingy, chipped paint to the freshly coated white from yesteryear and then filled the room with her mother's old furniture—still neatly encased in plastic.

"This place has a lot of happy memories." She turned toward the hall and caught an image of her father hunched over with her and Roslyn hanging around his neck and begging to be the first for a piggyback ride. If she remembered correctly, Sam won the battle since she took up the tactic of clinging around his leg so he couldn't walk.

Leila moved from one room to another, besieged by memories and haunted by distant laughter from so long ago. Sam had been right. There was a strange peace about the house—despite the fact it looked like the perfect locale for a horror movie.

When it came time to visit the last room—her mother's room—she stalled.

She shook her head and wiped at the few errant tears that streamed down her face. "I have to do this." She opened the door and was finally able to put the ghost of the past to rest.

It was close to midnight when she arrived home. It was late, probably too late to pay Garrick a visit—but she wanted to get this over with and there was no better time than now. She climbed out of her car and closed the door.

"I thought you weren't coming home."

Leila jumped. When she turned around, she came face to face with Garrick. "What are you doing here?"

He stepped out of the shadows and the night's full moon illuminated his handsome features. "I take it you're not happy to see me?"

"Actually, I'm thrilled."

Her response surprised him. When he finally recovered, he boldly erased the shallow distance between them. "I made a decision tonight," he said.

Leila fought to maintain her composure, but his closeness was playing havoc on her senses. "What kind of decision?"

Before she could blink, let alone think, Garrick kissed her. The mouth was hungry, possessive, and soul stirring all in one. Just when she was getting used to the taste of him, he pulled back.

"I decided that I love you."

"Garrick, I—"

"Let me finish," he said, drawing in a deep breath and erecting his towering frame. "I love you and I'm not going to let you get rid of me. You were right the last time. I can't offer any guarantees about the future—it's part of the mystique of falling in love."

Leila lowered her head as she reflected on the truth of his words.

Garrick's strong fingers gently lifted her chin and forced their eyes to meet. "Another component is that I am willing to compromise." With his free hand, he drew her pliant body against him. "I know motherhood has never been a part of your plans and I accept that."

"Garrick—"

"If you don't want children, then we won't have any. But one thing I will *not* do is become second fiddle to your job. If this is going to work, I'm going to be number one in your life. Just like you will be number one in mine—as my wife." His lips captured hers in another tantalizing kiss.

Wife? Leila melted as she slid her arms around his neck and pulled him closer. Until that moment, when the familiar heat and strength of his body pressed against hers again, she hadn't been sure if she was dreaming all of this. He'd come back to her without knowing about the baby.

Like before, the kiss ended too soon, but she continued to hold on to him for support.

"Does this mean we have a deal?" he asked.

"You want to marry me?"

"Weird, huh?"

She smiled. "Yeah, because what are the odds that I'd want to marry you, too?" She kissed him again. "Won't you come inside? There's something I need to tell you."

Chapter 26

"You're what?" Garrick's eyes bulged with incredulity, and then looked as though he needed to sit down. "Are you sure? When did this—when did you find out?"

Leila directed him to the sofa and urged him to take a seat. "I found out this afternoon. Ciara and Roslyn bought me a home pregnancy test."

"And it was positive?" he asked as if he were afraid to hope.

Leila's smile bloomed as she nodded.

"Woo-hoo!" Garrick leaped into the air. "I'm going to be a father!" He turned to her and pulled her into his arms and began bouncing around the room. Then just as suddenly, he realized what he was doing. "Oh, I'm sorry. You shouldn't be doing that." Gently but firmly, he directed her back down to the sofa. "Can I get you anything? Do you need some water or something?" He propped her feet up.

Leila burst out in giggles. "No. I don't need anything."

"Are you sure? It's late. Maybe I should get you to bed?"

Still fighting her laughter, she tugged his sleeve and made him sit down next to her. "Are you going to be like this during the whole pregnancy?"

"Like what?" he asked with wide-eyed innocence.

At that moment, he was the most adorable man she had ever seen. He glowed like a kid in a candy shop who was given his parents' platinum credit card. "Now, I know this isn't something you planned," he began. "But I want you to know that I'm more than willing to do most of the—"

"Shh. Shh." She placed a finger against his lips. "This baby is definitely a part of all my plans…and so are you." She kissed him and then smiled against his lips. "I hope you know what you're getting yourself into. Some people tend to think I'm a little neurotic."

"You don't say?"

"By the way, I sold my company."

"What? Why? I thought *Atlanta Spice* was your baby?"

She smiled warmly at him. "Well, I'm about to have a real baby…plus I have you."

"Backhanded compliment?"

"Just another wonderful service I provide." Leila wrapped her arms around his neck.

"But what will you do? You're not going to convince me that you want to spend the rest of your life as a housewife."

"No," she agreed. "I will still be working at *Atlanta Spice,* but no more than twenty hours a week and even that's flexible. This way I can have the best of both worlds."

"Are you sure this is what you want? I don't want you to do something you'll regret."

"The only thing I regret is lying to myself for so long. I learned a lot about myself today and I owe a lot of it to my family…and you. Now, how about we go upstairs and have makeup sex?"

"Can we…?" He glanced down at her belly. "Do you think that's a good idea?"

"What's the point of fighting if we don't get to have makeup sex?"

"I mean, do you think it will harm the baby?"

"I think the baby will be just fine." She drew him in for yet another kiss.

Garrick swooped her into his arms and carried her off to bed. Once they reached the bedroom, the lovers raced to tear off their clothes and fuse their bodies together.

Leila laughed, cried, and then laughed some more, while she remained in complete awe of how her man excited her body in ways only he knew how. How had she ever convinced herself that she could go through the rest of her life without this man? How had she convinced herself that a career was more important than family or love?

Sometime before dawn, the sated lovers lay spooned together and discussed their future.

"So…how many do you think we should have?" Garrick asked, nibbling on her earlobe.

"I don't know." She thought dreamily. "Maybe we should play it by ear?" She giggled.

"Sounds like a plan to me. Of course, we have to get the wedding out of the way. What are you doing next weekend?"

"Next weekend? You don't think that's a little fast?"

"All right. To show how flexible I am—how about in two weeks?"

"Now that's better. I think we can throw a little somethin' somethin' together in two weeks. We could either have it here or across the street?"

He snuggled closer. "Actually…I have a buyer for the house—but I do have this killer bachelor pad in Buckhead."

Leila jabbed her elbow into his side. "You mean the one you're about to get rid of?"

Garrick took the blow but then retaliated by

tickling her sides. All efforts to leap out of bed failed when he turned her over and pinned her beneath him.

"Do you give up?"

Giggling, she struggled to breathe. "Never."

He locked her hands above her head and rained kisses along the column of her neck. "How about now?"

"No. No," she cried and bucked with laughter.

Garrick's hot mouth abandoned the sweet plains of her neck to travel down the equally tantalizing valley of her breasts. She immediately stilled at the feel of his hardened desire pressed against her thigh. "What about now?" he asked again and then closed his mouth around her nipple.

Leila bucked and then sucked in a breath as he slid into her. He kept her hands pinned above her while their hips rocked in perfect unity. Tears slid from her eyes at the glorious feel of his slow, deliberate moves. She was suddenly overwhelmed when a fire lit within her and scorched her very soul.

"I love you," repeatedly tumbled from her lips while "Sweet Leila" fell from his. Her head thrashed among the pillows in wanton abandonment while Garrick's thrusts transformed into hard pounds. Together, they cried out as their bodies erupted and sent violent tremors of release through every inch of them.

Hot and slick with sweat, Garrick fell limp against her. "Never mind. I think *I* give up."

Leila chuckled and rolled him onto his side. "Good. Because I was just about to say it." She propped up on her side. "I know about the bid on the house. Sam and her husband Emmanuel placed it."

His brows dipped in confusion. "Husband? Sam and Emma are back in town?"

Leila nodded and quickly gave him the Cliff's Notes version of Samantha and Emmanuel. As she told the story, she was again struck by the similarities between her and Samantha's lives. Before, she had been convinced they were as different as night and day.

"Hey, where did you go?"

Garrick's voice bounced her out of her trance and she smiled sleepily up at him. "I was just thinking about Samantha."

He gently stroked the side of her face. "What about her?"

"I just hope that she's truly happy this time."

"What about you?" he asked. "Are you happy?"

"Oh, yes." She clung to him. "What about you?"

He smiled wickedly. "How about I show you?"

Two weeks later, Garrick Grayson stood before the minister in Leila's backyard, waiting anxiously for his future. It was his second time at the altar and he was certain this time he'd gotten it right.

The "Wedding March" began and Leila made her grand entrance into the backyard dressed in a stunning strapless, pearl-beaded wedding dress and showcasing a smile that squeezed Garrick's heart.

Leila inhaled and exhaled slowly in order to calm her racing heart. All eyes were on her, but Leila only noticed Garrick's smoldering gaze. The ceremony went without a hitch; Leila's favorite part was their vows to love, honor, and cherish each other for the rest of their lives.

Those words had once sounded so foreign

and unrealistic. Now with Garrick, they sounded like an effortless task that she looked forward to doing for the rest of her life.

"Ladies and gentlemen, I now present to you Mr. and Mrs. Garrick Grayson."

Epilogue

Three months later

Leila nervously held Garrick's hand while the ultrasound tech squirted cold gel around her belly. Neither of them had gotten much sleep the past week, knowing today they would get to hear and see their baby.

"I can't wait." Leila squirmed, her eyes glued to the monitor.

"That makes two of us." Garrick kissed her temples and also kept his eyes on the monitor.

"Oh, my." The tech squinted at the small black-and-white screen.

"What is it?" Leila and Garrick asked in mild panic.

"Well, how do you two feel about having more than one baby?"

"Twins?" Garrick jumped to his feet. "We're going to have twins?"

Leila stared dumbfounded at him.

"Try triplets," the tech corrected and proceeded to point out her findings.

When she finished, Garrick let out a loud, "Woo-Hoo," grabbed the tech and spun her around the room. "Three!" He set her down and pivoted toward his wife. "Three, baby. Can you believe it? Baby?"

Leila had fainted.

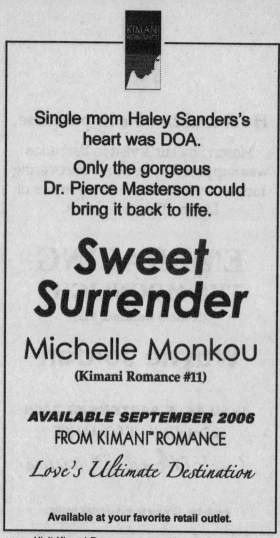

**Introducing an exciting appearance
by legendary
New York Times bestselling author**

DIANA PALMER

HEARTBREAKER

He's the ultimate bachelor…
but he may have just met
the one woman to change his ways!

Join the drama in the story of a confirmed
bachelor, an amnesiac beauty and their
unexpected passionate romance.

"Diana Palmer is a mesmerizing storyteller
who captures the essence of what
a romance should be."—*Affaire de Coeur*

**Heartbreaker *is available from Silhouette Desire
in September 2006.***